Mu[illegible] the Gelateria

Cala d'Oro Mysteries - Book 1

Victoria Amarin

WORLD BRIDGE PUBLISHING

World Bridge Publishing

This novel is entirely a work of fiction. The names, characters and incidents portrayed in it are the work of the author's imagination. Any resemblance to actual persons, living or dead, events or localities is entirely coincidental.

First edition

For anyone who's ever stood at the shore's edge and felt the sea quietly listen back.

Contents

Prologue

If you'd asked me two years ago where I'd be, I would have answered without hesitation: a glass-walled office in Milan, combing through financial records and corporate statements, searching for the cracks no one else wanted to admit were there. I was a forensic finance consultant, called in when reputations and millions of euros hung in the balance. My life was flights and hotel rooms, deadlines that stretched past midnight, and conference calls that blurred across time zones. My world smelled of antiseptic lobbies, pressed suits, and endless cups of burnt espresso in paper cups.

People in Milan used to call me *la ragazza con lo sguardo affilato* — the girl with the sharp gaze. Hazel eyes that could catch when a decimal point had been shifted, or when a partner's hands shook just enough during a meeting to betray the lie on his lips. I learned to carry myself like someone who already knew the answer to the question you were about to ask. It wasn't vanity. It was armor, and it served me well in boardrooms where the air was thick with ambition and fear.

Then Nonna died.

For as long as I could remember, she was the soul of gelateria Dolce Vita — a place that seemed to belong to another time. The shutters were sea-green and weathered, creaking in the Mediterranean breeze. The striped awning snapped like a sail whenever the *sirocco* blew through the *piazza*. Tourists found it by instinct, guided by the scent of sugar and cream. Locals stayed loyal because of Nonna's pistachio gelato: nutty, velvety, with the faintest trace of salt, the taste of land meeting sea. As a child, I spent summers behind that counter, barefoot on cool terrazzo tiles, skin sticky from hazelnut cones, hair tangled from salt spray. The air was thick with brine and sunlight, and my world was measured in scoops, not spreadsheets.

When she passed, she left me a ring of tarnished brass keys and the burden of choice. I told myself I would sell it. I wasn't the type to scoop gelato anymore, not when I had built a career on numbers and deception. But the truth was more complicated.

When I came down to Cala d'Oro to "handle the paperwork," the sea reached me first. It was in the salt on the breeze, in the cries of gulls circling the harbor, in the pastel glow of buildings leaning together as if sharing secrets. The *piazza* opened before me like a stage I thought I had left long behind. For the first time in years, I felt...still. And uneasy, though I didn't want to admit it.

I traded my suits for cotton dresses, my heels for sandals, my calendars for the rhythm of the tides. Yet some mornings, my hand still reached for a phone buzzing with meetings that would never come. I told myself I was stepping into a quieter life, a life made of mornings at the marble counter, afternoons of espresso steam and laughter in the *piazza*, evenings when the scent of lemon blossoms drifted in through open windows.

But I should have known better. Trouble does not disappear when you leave Milan. It follows you, finds you, sometimes waits for you.

Trouble has a way of finding you in Cala d'Oro. Especially here.

Chapter 1

Three Scoops

The gulls were already holding court above the harbor when I turned the key in Dolce Vita's front door. Their raucous cries bounced off the facades of the pastel buildings that clutched the curve of Cala d'Oro, a mosaic of peeled paint and sun-dulled shutters just waking up to another day. A few early risers, Signor Bardi shuffling his broom across the terrazzo of the wine shop, Marzia at her flower stall rearranging bruised zinnias, raised their heads to see who I was and whether I was worth a nod. I was not, apparently. In this town, I was background still. A necessary shape in the morning landscape, but not yet important enough to warrant acknowledgment.

Inside the gelateria, it was cool and shadowy, the air still clung to last night's chill. The little bell over the door gave a nervous jangle at my entrance, as if surprised to be called to duty so early in the season. I paused just inside, hands on hips, surveying the narrow room with its lineup of mirrored tables, pale terrazzo floor, and glass case still dark and lifeless.

The sound of my own breath was unexpectedly loud. For a second, I remembered the silence of winter here, the weeks when the wind howled so ferociously off the water it felt like the whole town might slip off the *faccia della terra* and disappear. But now, in May, the world was blooming: muggy salt air, yeast from the bakery across the *piazza*, and the faintest trace of last night's cypress smoke. I opened the door wide and propped it with the rusty iron gelato cone, letting the scents and the morning sunlight chase away the shadows.

Through the window the tide glittered beyond the *piazza,* reminding me of the walk I'd promised myself before evening. A stretch of sand, a pocket of shells — Nonna had called it "medicine for the soul." I still brought home the curved and pitted ones, tucking some of them also into jars behind the counter, quiet reminders of where the town met the sea.

I set about my opening ritual, which I had refined into a choreography of small, precise movements: switch on the overhead lights, set the espresso machine to warming, prepare the lemon water and arrange it alongside the stack of mismatched glasses, each with its own chip or spiderweb crack. I had made it a point not to fix the glassware. The regulars expected to see their signatures in the vessels, a kind of tactile proof of daily life.

The freezer hummed to life beneath my palm, and a mechanical click told me the glass case was ready to illuminate its treasures. Beside it, a smaller cabinet displayed pastries — *bomboloni* and *cornetti* delivered from the bakery on the corner, biscotti in jars, and the occasional tray of almond cake I baked myself when the mood struck. A narrow shelf behind the counter carried the little extras I'd started offering last summer: jars of melon marmalade with hand-written labels, cones of candied almonds, and cotton tote bags printed with Dolce Vita's name in looping script. Not exactly a full souvenir stand, but enough to please tourists who wanted to carry a piece of the shop home.

The coffee machine rattled as it warmed, a plain two-lever model that pulled a sturdy espresso or a foamy caffè latte, nothing more. My years in Milan had spoiled me — I had grown used to cortados in glass cups, cappuccinos dusted with cinnamon, and the parade of newer fads that seemed to change with the seasons: matcha or pumpkin spice lattes, chai with oat milk, even pistachio cream folded into foam.

Sometimes the tourists asked. A woman from London once leaned across the counter and whispered as if it were contraband, "Do you do flat whites?" Another had wanted almond milk, and a German family had looked at me hopefully asking about matcha latte when I explained the only edible green thing in the shop was pistachio gelato. I smiled, apologized, and pulled them an espresso instead. Most of them forgave me once the gelato case lit up and they tasted what Dolce Vita really offered.

The fishermen and pensioners of Cala d'Oro never asked for anything different. They wanted their familiar espresso, quick and black, served in the chipped cups they'd known for years. And if I was honest, I preferred it that way. The shop wasn't Milan, and I had no desire to turn it into a branch of some international coffee chain. The sea was just down the street, the air smelled of salt and lemons — who needed turmeric foam on top of that?

Around me the gelateria woke as well, the small round tables with their wrought-iron legs, the chairs painted white long ago and worn smooth at the edges by countless hands. Along one wall hung framed photographs from the fifties and sixties, my Nonna in a starched apron smiling beside tubs of gelato, the *piazza* behind her unchanged except for the hairstyles. Faded bunting, strung for some festival years ago, still clung stubbornly to the ceiling beams, and I had never found the heart to take it down. The room smelled faintly of coffee grounds, orange peel, and sugar, a mixture that told its own history as clearly as any recipe book.

In Milan, my mornings had the sour, metallic tang of vending machine coffee and the ozone bite of the photocopier. Here, I got the jewelry-box moment every day: lifting the brushed steel lid and seeing rows of gelato, still velvety and perfect, in colors that would embarrass a gemstone dealer. Pistacchio, so green it looked radioactive. *Amarena*, streaked with crimson-colored cherry. Stracciatella, pristine like snowy peaks, marbled with chocolate shards.

Dolce Vita had been my Nonna's before it was mine, and though I kept her classic flavors like hazelnut, stracciatella, the lemon that stung the tongue like sun on salt, I'd also inherited her mischief. Nonna used to say every summer needed one surprise, something nobody expected but everyone remembered. Her notebooks, stained with syrup and gelato drips, were full of experiments: fig with thyme, orange with basil, even one attempt at anchovy that the town teased her about for a very long time. I'd picked up where she left off, testing a new twist every now and then. Today's trial was rosemary–pear, earthy and sweet, waiting in the smallest metal tub at the back of the case. Few would dare it, but I liked having it there, like a secret between Nonna and me.

I made an extra effort smoothing the surfaces today, even though I knew I would have to do it again before customers arrived. It was a silly impulse, an aesthetic tic. Maybe it was genetic; my mother always said presentation was ninety percent of a meal, no matter how poor you were. I used the long-handled spatula to draw a little swirl in the *nocciola*, then stepped back to admire the effect. Not bad, I thought. Not bad at all.

Just as I finished aligning the sugar cones in their holder, I heard a familiar throat-clearing from the sidewalk. Too early for the schoolchildren, and the fisherman crowd never came this far up the hill before lunch. That left only one possible candidate.

Lucia appeared at the doorway with the timing that comes from decades of monitoring the town's rhythms. Her silver hair was wrapped in a lemon-patterned scarf, and she carried a wicker basket suspiciously empty for someone claiming to be "just passing by." No doubt she had been perched at her window since dawn, watching for my lights to flicker on, the same way she tracked the fishermen's boats and the mayor's morning walks.

She paused at the terracotta planter outside, tsking under her breath as she plucked a few yellowed leaves from the geraniums.

"Look at this. The wind has been too rough for them this week." She pinched off a sprig of rosemary, held it to her nose, and smiled. "Perfect for potatoes, if you don't overdo it."

Her hand drifted to a cluster of pale pink blossoms on the next plant. "Oleandro. Pretty enough, but it will make you sick if you are careless. Even the goats know better." She tossed the bit into the bin without ceremony, then pointed to a struggling basil plant tucked in beside the door. "And this one...hopeless. Needs more sun. I will bring you a cutting from mine next week."

I leaned against the counter, smiling despite myself. "You don't miss much, do you?"

Lucia's eyes crinkled. "Not in this town. You can learn everything worth knowing just by watching. Except about yourself. That you have to hear from your neighbors, whether you like it or not."

Before I could answer, she tilted her head toward the *piazza*. "Ah, and here comes Marco, trying to look important."

Sure enough, Marco Rossi, my childhood friend and now Cala d'Oro's policeman, strode confidently across the sunlit square, his uniform crisp. The polished buttons reflected the light, casting tiny glimmers as he moved, giving him an air that was both authoritative and faintly ridiculous at the same time.

"Pistachio," he declared as soon as he reached the counter, his voice firm and decisive, as if issuing a police command.

"It's not even ten in the morning," I laughed, raising an eyebrow at his unusual choice of breakfast.

He leaned one elbow on the counter as though he had all the time in the world. "Some people start the day with coffee. I start mine with taste tests. Quality control," he explained, as if it were the most logical thing in the world.

"One of these mornings I'll give you basil with cherry instead of pistachio, just to see if you notice." I laughed.

Lucia sniffed, though not unkindly. "You will never find a wife if you keep eating like that," she chided gently, her eyes twinkling.

Marco grinned. "Maybe I am not looking for a wife, *Zia* Lucia. Maybe I am just looking for the best pistachio in Italy. And I know where to find it." He tapped the glass counter with his forefinger.

I scooped, trying not to laugh, and handed him the cone. "You know you are going to put me out of business if you keep demanding samples every morning."

"Then consider it my civic duty," he smiled, biting off the tip in one sharp movement. He chewed, narrowed his eyes as though conducting a serious investigation, and then gave a solemn nod. "Better than last week. Maybe just a touch less bitter?"

I bent closer, mock-conspiratorial. "That's the point. Real Sicilian pistachios, none of that green-dyed powder from Naples."

Marco chuckled. "Spreadsheets and smugglers. That's your kind of crime scene, isn't it?"

I pretended to polish the counter. "Don't tempt me. I walked away from all that."

He studied me for a beat too long, his expression hovering between teasing and something more curious. I told myself not to read into it. Marco had always been easy on the eyes, in the way small-town golden boys often are. But easy was dangerous, and I had already had enough of dangerous men in sharp suits and charming grins.

He shrugged the moment off. "Well, you are safer here. The only crime in Cala d'Oro is me stealing gelato from you."

Patting my arm Lucia added, "...and gossip! Do not forget gossip. It is faster than any thief." She gave Marco a look as though he were a mischievous child, and then shuffled toward the door with her basket swinging.

By late morning, the tempo had changed. The shadow from the awning fell diagonally across the terrazzo, slicing the shop in two: a shady wedge near the register, and a growing pool of gold around the door, where customers gathered like moths stunned by light.

Children were the first to arrive, clutching coins and sticky with anticipation. I knew them all by name, which was not much of an accomplishment in Cala d'Oro, but it felt like one to me. Their vividness, their stubborn little rituals, made me wish I could remember what it felt like to want something that badly.

In the late afternoon, the next wave came with the tourists: German cyclists in Lycra, Dutch couples in their matching linen hats, squinting at my chalkboard menu and mustering a few brave syllables of Italian. They always ordered the classics, limone, fragola, vaniglia, careful not to venture into the unfamiliar. I overheard their comments as they tasted, that same delighted surprise, as if they had not believed a town this small could do anything right. Sometimes I wanted to tell them about my own surprise at winding up here, that their discovery was only a tiny echo of my own.

For a moment, I allowed myself to feel it: a fragile sense of safety. Between the clatter of spoons, the chatter of children, and the tourists fumbling with coins, it felt like the world was, if not perfect, at least steady. Even Marco's earlier grin, lingering too long over the counter, replayed in the back of my mind like a song I could not shake.

I caught myself smoothing the surface of the *amarena* gelato again, making an unnecessary swirl just to steady my hands. Old instincts, the kind that told me life rarely stayed simple for long.

Once more, the door announced a newcomer.

The man in the doorway wore a cream-colored linen suit that clung to his body like a damp shroud. Sweat darkened the collar, and his Italian leather shoes, easily worth a week of my earnings, bore the scars of a man who believed money exempted him from care. He dabbed his lips with a handkerchief, as though the heat, or something he had drunk or eaten, was not sitting well. His eyes, cold as January sea, swept over my gelato case with the merciless scrutiny of an executioner selecting his blade.

"*Buongiorno*," I managed, my throat suddenly dry. "Hot day, isn't it?"

His lips twitched into something that resembled a smile the way a shark resembles a dolphin. "Scorching enough to drive lesser men to pistachio. Not me." He stabbed his finger at three flavors. "Those. Now."

I scooped with my suddenly trembling hands, the dish rattling as I slid it across. He dissected each flavor with surgical precision, his silver pen slashing across his notebook like a knife. The shop fell tomb-silent, customers frozen mid-bite, their eyes magnetized to the spectacle.

His pen stabbed the air, suspended. A grimace seized his face. Then violently he clutched his chest, knuckles whitening. His eyes bulged in terror.

The spoon crashed to the floor, the sound like a gunshot in the silence.

Time fractured. Then chaos erupted, shouts ricocheting off walls, questions firing, a woman's shriek slicing through the pandemonium.

"Marco!" someone called out to the street, and as if summoned by the panic in their voice, he appeared in the doorway, pushing through the crowd with practiced authority.

My heart hammered against my ribs. This was not just drama. This was catastrophe unfolding in my shop while the late afternoon sun still blazed through the windows, casting long shadows across what should have been the busiest hours of the day.

Chapter 2

Fatal Crossroads

The linen-suited man's body jerked sideways in a single, violent motion that stole the air from the room. His arms flailed, the chair screeched against the tiles, and both crashed to the floor in a tangle of limbs. In an instant, the gelateria transformed from ordinary daily chatter to a pocket of chaos. Marco dropped to one knee, sliding a hand beneath the man's head, the other tearing open buttons with crisp efficiency. His fingers pressed against the man's neck, searching. My own gaze strayed past him to the leather bag dangling from the toppled chair. Its flap gaped, and on top of a stack of papers lay an old photograph: a warehouse front, wooden crates stacked in neat rows, the image worn with time.

"Call an ambulance!" Marco ordered. His voice was not raised, but the command filled the space like thunder.

For a moment no one moved. The woman by the window pressed herself flat against the glass, clutching her little purse as if leather and stitching could keep her safe. The old man who had been reading *La Repubblica* lowered the paper, his eyes suddenly wide and wet. At the counter, a high-schooler I knew from his daily chocolate cone fumbled out his phone with trembling hands. Whether he was calling emergency services or recording a video, I couldn't tell.

For one strange, suspended moment, it seemed possible the man might rise, dust himself off, and mutter an apology. Instead, a strangled whine broke from his throat, thin and wet, and his skin blanched to the sickly pallor of curdled milk.

"Not here," Marco hissed. "Out. All of you."

The old man shuffled for the exit. The woman clung to the wall as she sidled past. The boy stood frozen, mouth slack, until Marco's glare jolted him into retreat.

I stayed rooted behind the counter, fingers gripping the edge of the glass until pain shot up my knuckles. My body refused every order I gave it: fetch water, clear space, bring something — anything. All I could do was breathe, and even that felt like a conscious act.

I stared at the man convulsing on the floor. His chest rose and fell too quickly, the sound of someone drowning in air itself. My mind raced back to the order: three scoops, chosen with that imperious jab of his finger. *Amarena, stracciatella*, lemon. Had there been nut traces? A residue from cleaning fluid? Some unnoticed error in preparation? I replayed the fine print of my menu in my head — "may contain traces of dreams or despair." It had been a joke when I wrote it. Now the words jeered back at me.

The sound of sirens swelled outside, slicing through the air, and then the doorway filled with fluorescent green. Three paramedics swarmed in, vests emblazoned with SOCCORSO. Marco stepped back, hands raised, as they descended in a well-practiced dance.

Pulse, monitor, injection. One unfurled a metallic blanket, another ripped open a plastic kit and drove a syringe into the man's thigh. Their Italian blurred together, but phrases leapt out. *Aritmia grave.* Severe arrhythmia. *Pressione bassa.* Blood pressure dropping. *Possibile intossicazione.* Possible poisoning.

"Something he ate," one muttered.

"Or drank," another corrected, her gaze sliding to the half-melted dish on the tiles.

The man's body shuddered once, then sagged. The paramedic with the clipboard glanced up, eyes briefly locking on mine, as if stamping my face into memory, before turning back to the beeping monitor.

Within minutes he was strapped to a stretcher, mouth slack beneath a clear mask. Tubes trailed behind as the team hustled him out, leaving the shop littered with wrappers and the acrid tang of antiseptic. When the door swung shut, silence pooled in their wake, deeper than before, as if even the freezer motor held its breath.

I stayed frozen, one hand still pressed to the counter, the other limp at my side. A puddle of gelato crept across the floor, pale cream and cherry red swirling together in a grotesque imitation of marble.

Marco rose, wiping his hands on his trousers. He crossed to me, his eyes steady. For a heartbeat I thought he might offer comfort. Instead, his voice came low, practical. “Clean up.”

The word landed like a slap. Still, my legs moved before my mind caught up. I pulled the mop from the closet and attacked the spill, movements sharp, too fast, as if speed alone could erase what had happened here. My reflection in the glass case was unrecognizable — face bloodless, hair plastered with sweat, eyes wide and rimmed red.

From the back room, Marco’s voice rumbled through the half-closed door, clipped and furious into his phone. I couldn’t make out the words, but the tone was enough.

When I turned, the boy with the chocolate cones still lingered, his phone dangling uselessly in his grip.

He edged closer. “Did he die?” His voice cracked low, as if straining for maturity.

“No,” I snapped, sharper than I intended. I forced my tone softer. “They’ll take care of him.”

He nodded, unconvinced, and slipped out, leaving the door still ajar.

The second the shop is empty, my legs threaten to fold. I brace myself against the counter, breathing in short, useless sips. Suddenly I felt out of place as never before. I want to call my mother in Frankfurt, or my sister, or anyone who will listen, but I don’t know what I’d say. I imagine the man’s family, the people at his office, the strangers who will read about it tomorrow and make judgments about the carelessness of foreigners, the incompetence of immigrants, even though my father’s from here and my Nonna is buried up the hill. I picture the headlines: FOREIGN GELATAIA HOSPITALIZES ELDERLY MAN. I picture myself behind bars, or worse, deported. The fantasy is so vivid that for a second I almost laugh.

The bell rang again. Relief flickered — another customer, maybe unaware, I thought. But it was not.

A man stepped inside in a navy uniform, badge glinting, notebook open. He was tall, but it was his presence that filled the room: suspicion etched into the creases of his mouth, sharp eyes scanning the mess before fixing on me. He did not introduce himself. The pen clicked in his hand, a brittle sound that made me flinch.

"Bianca Moretti?"

"Yes," I managed, though it sounded uncertain.

"You served him."

"Yes. Three scoops." I gestured to the congealed mess still staining the tiles.

"What flavors?"

"*Amarena, stracciatella*, lemon."

He scribbled without looking up. "Anyone else order the same combination?"

"No. Not together."

The notebook snapped shut. "We'll need samples."

"Samples?"

"Of the gelato." His gaze flicked to Marco, who had finished his call and slipped back in without my noticing. "Seal the premises."

My stomach plunged. "Wait, seal the premises? You can't—"

Marco's eyes held regret, but he took the roll of tape and stretched it across the doorway, yellow bands crisscrossing the sea-green shutters like a wound.

From the *piazza* came the sound I dreaded: voices. Rumor spreading like spilled wine. Cala d'Oro was built of stone and salt and centuries of stories. Sound bounced and multiplied here until gossip turned deafening.

"They say she poisoned him."

"She snapped, poor thing."

"Who knew gelato could kill?"

I pressed my forehead against the glass, the words clanging in my skull. I didn't need to see the faces to know who was speaking: *Signora* Bassi from the flowers, the newsstand twins, the butcher's wife. Each voice carried its own signature, twisting details as it passed.

By nightfall, three entirely different tales had already made the rounds. In the first, I had threatened the poor man with a gelato spatula and his heart had simply given out. In the second, I was said to have confused lemon syrup with cleaning solution, poisoning him by accident in some tragic act of incompetence. And in the third, the one that spread fastest among the morning regulars, the man hadn't died from gelato at all, but from "daylight robbery," the sheer shock of seeing my prices climb twenty cents since last summer.

I hugged my arms tight, almost laughing at the absurdity. The town's efficiency was terrifying; within hours the myth was already cementing, while the truth slipped further from reach. Tomorrow, the stories would be worse. By next week, my name could be splashed across national papers, or worse, mangled in some international clickbait.

Lucia appeared at dusk with a paper bag of pastries. She eyed the police tape with contempt.

"*Stronzi.* Fools," she muttered. "Half this town has eaten your gelato without trouble. It isn't the gelato."

I wanted to believe her. But the memory of the officer's eyes said otherwise.

Lucia leaned close, her floral perfume comforting. "That man, Claudio Vespucci. Food critic. *La Repubblica.*" Her voice dropped further. "This morning I saw him at the post office. He and Carlo were arguing like wild dogs. Carlo jabbing his finger, Vespucci red as a boiled octopus. Whatever happened to him, maybe it started there."

I swallowed, torn between dread and curiosity. "What are people saying now?"

Lucia's gaze softened, though her words did not. "That he was poisoned. And that it happened here."

It shouldn't have surprised me. The town had been whispering it since it happened. Hearing it stated like a fact only pressed the air tighter in my chest. I used to investigate with spreadsheets and audit trails, neat columns that balanced and never looked back at me. This was different. This was a man, a family, a town that would decide who I was by sundown. I could leave it to the police and pray they saw sense, or I could start the only way I know how: by tracing the man himself. Where he came from, what he touched, who he spoke to. If it wasn't my gelateria, then where? And if it really was poison, how had it reached him? I didn't feel ready for any of it. But if I wanted my shop back — and my name — then following Vespucci's trail was the only path ahead of me.

Lucia touched my arm. "Come. You shouldn't sit alone tonight."

We crossed the *piazza* to her building, a peach-colored facade with geraniums spilling from the balcony. From her second-floor window she had a clear view of the square, the flower stall, and most of the harbor road. "You don't need to leave your chair to know what's going on in this town," she smiled wryly, jangling her keys.

Inside, her kitchen smelled faintly of vinegar and herbs. Shelves of jars glinted ruby and green in the lamplight — peppers, zucchini, onions steeped in brine. She pulled one down and pressed it into my hands as if it were medicine. "Eat. Pickled things last through storms and scandals...eh, longer than men, usually. Keep it in your fridge. You'll see."

Chapter 3

Gulls of Gossip

I woke up the next morning late to the sound of gulls arguing outside my window, as if they'd been hired to provide commentary on my life.

There she is, the gelato killer!

Oh no, she's the one with the almond conspiracy!

If only I could bribe them with a scoop of pistachio to spread better rumors.

The tape across Dolce Vita's front door had been a punch to the gut last night. This morning it was a full-on stomach ache. No shop meant no sales, no sales meant no money, and no money meant I'd be back in Milan by Christmas — assuming anyone there would hire the woman who poisoned a food critic.

Last night, just before sunset, Marco stopped by, face unreadable. "They did everything they could," he muttered. "Vespucci died an hour ago at the Ravenna hospital."

The words lodged in my chest. It wasn't just an incident in my shop anymore. It was a death.

I made coffee strong enough to stand a spoon in, sat at my kitchen table, and stared at the old ceramic sugar jar that had belonged to Nonna. She'd have told me not to waste time feeling sorry for myself, to do something.

Well, I was doing something.

Lucia's comment from last night wouldn't leave me alone — she'd seen Vespucci arguing with Carlo Benedetti outside the post office. Carlo owned one of Cala d'Oro's fancier trattorie, all gleaming glassware and imported wines, and I'd known him since my teenage market days with Nonna. I had never liked the way he measured people with his eyes before deciding if they were worth speaking to. Now, with my shop shuttered and his name in the mix, I liked him even less. I threw on a sundress, sandals, and my most innocent smile, then headed down the street.

Cala d'Oro was already buzzing: fishermen bargaining at the harbor, tourists snapping photos of things locals ignored, children chasing a beach ball dangerously close to café tables.

From Trattoria Benedetti drifted the smell of frying anchovies, sharp and oily. From Inside, Carlo stood behind the counter, sleeves rolled to his elbows, polishing a wine glass with the focus of a man intent on disciplining it.

"Bianca!" His voice rang out, warm — too warm? I couldn't tell if it was genuine hospitality or the sort of welcome meant to soften me before the brush-off. Carlo and I had never been close, and suddenly his smile looked like it had more teeth than kindness.

"Come for lunch? You shouldn't stay hidden away at a time like this."

"I thought I'd support a fellow business owner," I announced lightly, slipping into a table by the window. If he thought I'd come for comfort, he'd be mistaken. "And maybe ask about something I heard."

The cloth stilled against the glass. Just for a second — but I saw it, I think.

"Oh?"

"Lucia mentioned she saw you and Vespucci having words yesterday."

Carlo's smile returned, practiced and smooth, but I could still feel the pause lingering behind it. "Arguing? We spoke, yes. Nothing of consequence. Business matters."

"Business matters that carried across the *piazza*?"

He gave a chuckle, all surface, no warmth, and turned toward the kitchen. "*Signora* Lucia has a talent for drama. You shouldn't take it too seriously."

I watched him retreat, wondering whether I was inventing shadows where there were none, or whether Carlo preferred the shadows because he already had something to hide.

Carlo returned from the kitchen balancing a plate of fried sardines, the scent of lemon and hot oil wafting across the room. He set it down with a flourish. "On the house," he declared, flashing a smile that showed too many teeth.

I hesitated before picking one up with the fork he'd laid beside the dish, but then just gave up and put worries aside. For a bit anyways. The batter was still sizzling faintly, crisp and golden, the fish inside soft enough to almost melt on my tongue. The sharpness of lemon cut through the oil, leaving a pleasant tang that clung to the roof of my mouth.

"Still the best in town," I sighed, and I meant it. My fork hovered over the plate again before I set it down. It felt strange to eat here, as if the act itself were a test I hadn't studied for.

Carlo folded his arms, proud and clearly pleased. "People talk, but they always come back to Benedetti's. Quality is quality."

I nodded, chewing slowly, watching him through lowered lashes. He looked relaxed enough — sleeves rolled, a dish towel slung over one shoulder, the easy rhythm of a man who had done this for decades. But beneath the surface, maybe, just maybe, something felt as if taut, like a violin string tuned a little too high.

When I circled back to Lucia's claim about his argument with Vespucci, he didn't deny it outright, merely adjusted his mustache and flashed a broad grin. *We were talking, yes. Nothing important.*

It sounded genuine. Too genuine maybe?

I speared another sardine, the batter flaking under the pressure of my fork. "Vespucci didn't seem exactly subtle," I said, letting the words hang between us. "If he had something against you, I imagine the whole *piazza* would have heard it."

Carlo chuckled, though the sound landed flat. "Bianca, you've been away too long and from your summers here, you may not even remember, anymore, but...this town loves its dramas. A raised voice rarely becomes a fistfight by morning. You know how it is."

Maybe I did. Maybe he was right. But as I chewed the last bite, I couldn't decide which unsettled me more — the possibility that Carlo was telling the truth, or that he was lying.

It wasn't much, but between the tight smile, the hazy answers, and the sudden generosity, I knew one thing: Carlo wanted me to think we were on the same side. And if Milan had taught me anything, it was that people who work this hard to win you over are usually hiding something.

As I stepped back out into the sunlight, I nearly collided with *Zia* Lucia, who was balancing two paper bags and wearing an expression of intense satisfaction.

"You look pleased with yourself," I observed, squinting my eyes suspiciously.

"I just came from the market. And I heard something you'll want to know." She paused, her eyes flicking over me as if weighing how much to share. "Your Nonna never turned anyone away," she added finally. "Not even me, and I was trouble in my youth. I owe her more than I could ever repay."

I blinked at the sudden shift, caught between gratitude and impatience.

"So when I see her granddaughter with trouble at the door, I'm not about to stand back and watch." She leaned closer, her voice dropping to a whisper. "Our critic friend was spotted at the harbor the day before he wandered into your shop. Vespucci was asking old Paolo about the cannery fire. Why anyone would bring that up after all these years is beyond me."

"One more thing," Lucia said, lowering her voice even more, "he was also inquiring about old photographs."

"Photographs?" I echoed, intrigued. The word made me pause. I thought of Vespucci's slumped on the chair that afternoon, the corner of that photo peeking out. The warehouse, the crates...I hadn't given it much thought at the time. Now, it seemed I should have.

She nodded, a mysterious smile playing on her lips. "Something related to the museum's collection, I believe. You should speak to Enzo. He knows everything about those dusty old boxes."

I had only exchanged pleasantries with Enzo Valli since my return, but two things were etched in my memory: his passion for history, and those captivating eyes that seemed to try to unravel secrets you didn't even know you held.

If Vespucci had been exploring the museum, perhaps Enzo could shed light on his intentions. And with a touch of fortune, I might finally receive a straightforward answer in this enigmatic town.

Chapter 4

First Impressions

By the time I reached Cala d'Oro's maritime museum, the sun was high enough to bake the cobblestones. Heat shimmered off the whitewashed walls, and the smell of the sea was sharper now, saltier, like the tide had turned while I'd been indulging Carlo's sardines. The cries of gulls bounced off the harbor, and every sound carried further in the heavy heat, children shrieking as they cannonballed off the pier, fishermen bellowing over the price of clams, the hollow clatter of café cups stacked for tourists who had yet to come from the beach.

The museum squatted at the far end of the harbor, a weathered building with blue shutters and a faded sign that simply read *Museo del Mare*. Nonna used to drag me here every summer afternoon when the sun was too strong for gelato to survive. I used to sulk on the steps until she bribed me with lemon granita. "One hour of history for one hour of sugar," she'd say, her hand firm on my shoulder. I would whine about "boring old boats" while secretly enjoying the stories about shipwrecks and storms, though I never admitted it. Back then, the museum had seemed cavernous. Now it looked like a stubborn relic, clinging to its patch of waterfront while the rest of the town dressed itself up for tourists.

I pushed the door open and stepped inside. Inside, the air was cooler but carried a faint tang of dust and varnish. Sunlight slanted through tall windows, catching motes that drifted lazily over displays of model ships, glass cases of shells, and black-and-white photographs of the harbor before there were espresso bars on every corner. A ship's bell dented with use sat in one corner, next to a jar of sea glass labeled *collected 1964*. Someone had once cared enough to catalogue even broken bottles polished by waves.

And there, leaning over a long table strewn with papers and a magnifying glass, was Enzo Valli.

I recognized him instantly, not because we'd spoken much since I'd moved back, but because Cala d'Oro is the kind of town where you know everyone's face, even if you don't know their business. Tall, dark hair swept back with a bit of silver on his temples, a few sun-lines at the corners of his eyes and a focus so complete he didn't notice me right away.

"*Buongiorno,*" I started, aiming for casual but hearing the slight catch in my own voice.

His head came up. For a heartbeat there was a flicker of recognition, then a slow smile. His eyes were the color of strong coffee, steady but unreadable. A day's stubble roughened his jaw, his rolled sleeves revealed forearms marked with faint, pale scars, the kind you earn, but not the kind you explain. He had a steadiness to him, but also something untamed, like the sea when it's calm only because it chooses to be.

"Bianca Moretti!" He exclaimed. "Haven't seen you in here since you were about...twelve? Thirteen? You used to sneak out into the courtyard whenever the guide droned on."

I laughed, startled. "I was eight. And the courtyard had shade."

"Excuses." His smile tugged sideways. "Do you still dislike being still?"

"Unfortunately for me, that's become my profession."

He chuckled and gestured to the table. "Your grandmother was right to bring you here. History has a way of explaining the present. Sometimes even the future."

I stepped closer, eyeing the spread of old photographs. Fishing boats with peeling paint. Men in flat caps mending nets. Women in long skirts hauling baskets of clams. Cala d'Oro looked rougher in those images, less polished for visitors.

"I heard you're the one to ask about photographs?" I looked at him.

His smile tilted. "That depends. Are we talking family snapshots or something more...complicated?"

"Complicated. Do you know Claudio Vespucci?"

"The food critic? I heard he collapsed yesterday. At your shop?"

I resisted the urge to roll my eyes. "Yes, and now half the town thinks I poisoned him. I'm trying to work out why he was here in the first place."

Enzo folded his arms, leaning back against the table. "And you came to me because...?"

"Because Lucia says he was asking about the old cannery fire and about photographs in the museum's collection. And you're the one who knows what's in those dusty boxes."

That earned me a quiet chuckle. "She's not wrong about the dust. Wait here."

He moved to a wall of weathered cabinets, pulling open drawers with practiced hands. While he searched, I drifted through the displays. A ship's wheel scarred by salt. Rusted compasses. A child's drawing of a boat, crayon-faded, pinned under glass. I pressed my hand briefly against the rugged wood of a model trawler, remembering how Nonna once told me, "Every net has holes, Bianca. The trick is knowing where they are."

Enzo returned with a thick file and big carton box. "The fire destroyed machinery, inventory, offices. But some of their archived documents, like the financial records, were stored elsewhere, so they survived."

I ran a finger across the cover. "And ended up here?"

"After the company folded, they went to town hall. Years later, they were dumped here. The collection's incomplete, but sometimes fragments tell more than whole stories."

He spread a dozen photographs across the table, the edges yellowed. I scanned them, and my breath caught when one leapt out — a sunny day in Cala d'Oro's harbor, probably the late 1980s or 90s judging by boxy Fiats crammed along the quay.

I knew this photo. The wooden crates stacked in neat rows. This was the same one I saw in Vespucci's bag when it fell onto my terrazzo floor. In the chaos of his collapse, my mind had registered it as a gloomy warehouse, but here, in the clear light of day, I saw it for what it was: Cala d'Oro's old cannery, buzzing with life on a busy afternoon.

"He wanted to see these?" I asked, my voice tighter than I intended. Enzo nodded. "He came by a couple of times last week. Said he was tracing old supply chains for a 'heritage food' piece he was working on. He spent more time with the photographs than the ledgers, but he asked to see both."

He laid out half a dozen photos across the table, each mounted on cardboard backing. My breath caught once again. In one, taken on a sunny day, my grandfather stood front and center, a rare smile creasing his weathered face, his arm slung around a lean man with a mischievous grin.

"Do you know who that is?" I asked, pointing.

Enzo glanced, then at me. "You don't?"

I shook my head.

"That's Matteo Rossi. Fisherman, handyman, general troublemaker. Died in the cannery fire."

I blinked. "The same fire Carlo Benedetti was involved in as I heard?"

"Yes. Officially, it was faulty wiring. But plenty whispered Matteo was careless...or worse. His family always said he was scapegoated, but the gossip never died down."

I hesitated. "His family?"

Enzo's gaze blurred. "Marco's uncle. He doesn't advertise it, but everyone remembers. He was just a boy at the time, but he's lived under the shadow ever since. If Vespucci was digging into the fire, you can imagine Marco might prefer the past stay buried."

The idea hit me hard. Marco, carrying the weight of a family tragedy all these years, now tied —

however unfairly — to a scandal Vespucci had been sniffing at.

I traced a finger along the photo's edge. "So Vespucci was stirring old ghosts."

"Looks that way."

We sifted next through a box of cannery records. Pay slips, supplier letters, invoices. To most people, dull. To me, they were welcome puzzle pieces. My eye caught a loose scrap of paper tucked between the ledgers: a torn notebook page, with a column of dates and initials. One was underlined hard enough to dig the pen into the paper.

"August 15, 1990 – M.R.," I murmured. "That was a day before the fire."

Enzo leaned closer. "Matteo Rossi. That timing...it's strange."

Before I could answer, a shadow filled the doorway. Lucia, carrying a bag slung over her arm.

"Well, well. Leave you alone for an hour and you're knee-deep in trouble," she pronounced, looking at me with a twinkle in her eyes.

"How did you —"

"I had a feeling," she said tapping the side of her nose with a smile. "And I brought figs. And gossip." She plopped the bag on the table. "Carlo's been pacing his trattoria all morning like a cat on a hot stove."

Enzo frowned. "Interesting."

I tugged off the gloves Enzo had handed me earlier, shaking the dust from my fingers. "If Carlo knew Vespucci was digging into the fire — and that Matteo Rossi was tied up in it — maybe he feared Vespucci would piece some things together. At least some of it, things that slipped past before."

Lucia's eyes lit up, quick to fan the spark. "Then you'd best see what's on the stove before it boils over, eh?"

Enzo gave me a wry look. "You're really going to keep poking this, aren't you?"

"Yes," I responded simply. "Because if I don't, I'll be the one everyone's whispering about for the next thirty years. And...if I don't find out what happened to Vespucci, I wouldn't just lose a season's income, I'd lose the only home I'd built for myself since leaving Milan."

Chapter 5

Behind the Smile

The scent reached me before I turned the corner —garlic, rosemary, and the subtle smokiness of something lightly seared over an open flame.

In Cala d'Oro, you could follow your nose to the nearest meal, but this was richer, bolder. Almost like Carlo Benedetti's trattoria was daring the *piazza* to notice him.

It was my second visit in the last few days. The first time, he'd been all easy smiles and fried sardines "on the house." This time, I was here for more than lunch.

Trattoria Benedetti sat on a shady corner off the main square, the striped red-and-white awning fluttering in the sea breeze. The sign above the door had faded gracefully over decades, the elegant wrought iron outdoor tables and chairs arranged with the kind of effortless style only small Italian towns pull off.

I stepped inside, letting my eyes adjust to the dim cool. The air was thick with roasted peppers and simmering tomatoes. Behind the bar, Carlo stood with a phone pressed to his ear, his free hand drumming a restless rhythm on the counter. When he saw me, the conversation ended abruptly.

"Bianca," his smile arriving just a fraction late. "Lunch? Coffee?"

"Lunch," I clarified, sliding into a table by the window. "Somewhere I can see the *piazza*."

He gestured broadly. "Any table you like."

"I'll have the grilled sardines," I ordered after a glance at the menu.

One eyebrow lifted. "Popular choice today."

"Funny," I intoned lightly. "I didn't think sardines were in season."

For a heartbeat, something in his expression tightened. Then came the practiced shrug. "Frozen. Good quality." He vanished into the kitchen.

From my seat, I could see two old men bent over a card game of *maraffa*, German tourists clustered around a guide's yellow flag, and a boy splashing his hands in the fountain while his mother scolded half-heartedly.

Then Enzo Valli appeared. He leaned casually against the fountain, arms folded and holding a file. When he caught my gaze, he gave a subtle nod as if to say, *Stay calm,* before crossing the *piazza* and stepping inside. The door groaned softly, announcing his arrival a moment later.

"Mind if I sit?" he asked smoothly, glancing at us. "I'll have whatever pasta's on special today."

Before I could answer, Carlo interrupted, waving his hands. "We're a bit busy —"

"It's okay," I cut in, a little too quickly. "Have a seat."

Enzo slid into the chair opposite mine, casual as ever, though his eyes were sharper than his tone. "the other day, I was just telling Bianca about an interesting find at the museum," he noted, dropping the file on the table while reaching for bread.

Carlo's gaze flicked between us.

"A photograph," Enzo went on, pointing to the file he brought and breaking the crust cleanly. "From the nineties. The harbor. I imagine you'd have been around then."

Carlo's laugh didn't reach his eyes. "I suppose so. Memory's a bit hazy."

"It had Matteo Rossi in it," I remarked, keeping my tone light. "You remember him?"

A flicker in his gaze. "Matteo was a troublemaker. Got himself killed in that cannery fire. End of story."

"Stories don't end that neatly," I murmured.

A girl in a plain apron appeared with glasses on a tray, balancing them carefully. Her hands trembled just enough to make them click together. "My niece, Maria," Carlo explained, with a dismissive wave of his hand. She dipped her head quickly, her eyes fixed on the floor as she set the glasses before us.

But as she turned to leave, her gaze flickered up — not to my face, but to the folder of photographs on the table beside us. It was a fleeting look, but it held a weight of recognition, of fear. Then, her eyes darted toward the kitchen, door where Carlo's voice boomed, and she scurried away.

Later, as she brought the main course, her movements were less nervous, more deliberate. When she reached for my plate, her hand briefly, accidentally-on-purpose, nudged my water glass. As she apologized and mopped up the small spill with her cloth, her eyes finally met mine directly. It was only for a second, but the message in them was clear: a silent, desperate plea. It was gone in an instant, replaced by the blank mask of a server, but the connection was made. She knew I was digging, and she was watching.

The plates set before us were small works of art. My sardines glistened with char, flecked with lemon zest and parsley. The skin crunched under my fork, the flesh beneath melting with a sweetness that surprised me. A squeeze of charred lemon lifted the richness until it tasted almost like summer itself. For a moment I was eight years old again, perched on a stool in Nonna's kitchen while she fried fish in oil that crackled like a radio left on low.

Enzo's *pasta alle vongole* arrived steaming, fragrant with garlic, chili, and white wine. He twirled his fork, tasting a clam with a deliberate slowness before his mouth twisted into a half-smile. "At least the clams don't dodge questions."

I bit back a smile, focusing instead on the sardines, though the food couldn't distract me from Carlo's presence. He lingered too long nearby.

"Why are you two so interested in old photos?" he finally asked.

"Because Claudio Vespucci was interested," I said. "He had one in his bag when he collapsed in my shop."

Carlo's jaw tightened. "That's a shame," he responded flatly. Then, suddenly leaning in, "*Signorina* Moretti, *Signor* Valli, you're playing with fire. Let it go."

A crash erupted from the kitchen — ceramic shattering on tile — and Carlo muttered something sharp before disappearing behind the door.

"That was subtle," I murmured.

"He's rattled," Enzo said.

"And rattled people make mistakes."

We ate in silence after that, but it wasn't comfortable. The trattoria's elegance, the soft clink of glasses, the delicate plating — none of it could smooth over the tension left hanging at the table.

Maria, Carlo's niece we saw earlier, cleared the plates with careful hands, but her eyes stayed on the floor. When Carlo glanced her way, she seemed to flinch as if the air itself had shifted, then retreated to the kitchen without a word. She returned with dessert: a slice of *torta della nonna,* dusted with powdered sugar, pine nuts gleaming. "Compliments of the house," she murmured, eyes never meeting mine.

I cut into the custard-soft center. Sweet, nutty, faintly lemony. Enzo took a bite, then leaned back, studying me with a faint smile. "If he's bribing us with *torta*, he's worried."

"Or he's confident enough to think sugar covers everything," I said, half-seriously.

We lingered over espresso, thick and dark, sipping slowly as the trattoria hummed with soft conversation.

I studied him. "Why are you really here, Enzo?"

He studied me for a moment, his eyes held mine, his gaze steady. He set his spoon down, fingers brushing the stem of his water glass. "Because Vespucci came to the museum before he died. He was digging into the cannery fire, asking for photographs, payroll records, names. Things that don't get pulled out unless someone wants to stir up trouble. I've lived here long enough to know who benefits from silence. And Carlo — he's been tied to that story for years, always turning up on the edges of it. Maybe I ignored it before. But now? With Vespucci dead and your shop caught in the middle, I can't."

I brushed a crumb off my dress, stalling. "So you decided to stalk me?"

"I decided you shouldn't go alone," he said, then paused. "Not this time." I looked at him, but he didn't elaborate. His gaze didn't waver.

The words shouldn't have landed the way they did, but my pulse betrayed me. Around us, the trattoria hummed with easy chatter, but the air between us felt charged.

After we drank the coffee quickly we stepped into the sunlit *piazza*. The air outside was heavier, the sky faintly bruised with the promise of a storm. We walked side by side, the space between us just wide enough to keep things from tipping into something else.

"Do you think they'll talk?" I asked.

"They already are," he said. "But I'm not worried about them." For a second, I wondered if he meant the townspeople. Or something else entirely.

Enzo shoved his hands in his pockets, the movement drawing my attention to the strong line of his shoulders beneath his linen shirt. "He's hiding something."

"Of course he is. The question is, how do we make him talk?"

A gull shrieked overhead, wheeling low before settling on the fountain's edge. I followed its arc until Enzo's voice pulled me back.

"You're enjoying this, aren't you?"

I hesitated, caught between denial and truth. "Maybe a little," I admitted, sharper and more defensively than I meant to.

He tilted his head, the ghost of a smile tugging at his mouth. "You sound like Milan Bianca, not gelato Bianca."

Milan. The word lodged in my chest, stirring memories I'd tried to leave behind. The late nights of sorting figures, chasing names through records, seeing patterns where no one else looked. I shouldn't feel that old rush now, not with my shop's reputation at stake. But I did — and the admission unsettled me almost as much as Benedetti's warning.

Around us, the piazza moved on, oblivious. Yet standing there with Enzo, it felt like we were sharing secrets no one else could hear. A ripple of déjà vu swept through me — the same pull I'd known in Milan, when puzzles seemed to open just for me. The instincts I thought I'd buried were stirring again, half thrill and half dread. And beneath it all, I sensed this was only the beginning.

Chapter 6

Figs and Fires

The storm came earlier than expected. By mid-afternoon, Cala d'Oro's turquoise skies had thickened into a patchwork of slate-colored clouds, and the air pressed against my skin like damp wool. Fishermen at the harbor hurried to cover their boats, the metallic clink of chains and the slap of canvas echoing over the water. Thunder rolled low across the horizon, the kind that vibrated in your bones and promised the storm wasn't far off.

I couldn't bear the silence of the shuttered gelateria any longer. I packed two slices of almond cake into a bag and walked into the *piazza*, skirts plastered to my legs in the rising wind and early showers of rain.

Lucia opened her door before I knocked, her favorite lemon-print scarf slipping loose around her shoulders. "You'll drown out there," she said briskly, pulling me inside.

Her kitchen smelled of vinegar, figs, and rain, jars lined the shelves. On the table, she was quartering plump figs, their ruby pulp bleeding onto the board. She slid a small plate toward me, the fruit drizzled with honey and scattered with pine nuts. "Eat. Storms go easier with something sweet."

As I bit into one, Lucia's knife kept moving. "Carlo Benedetti received a delivery this morning. A crate. Large enough for two men to stagger with it, and not a label in sight. No wine branding or fish supplier mark. Nothing."

I frowned. "*Zia* Lucia, but restaurants take deliveries every day! Fresh produce, pasta —"

"Not like this one," she cut in, shaking her head. "And one of the men...tall, thin, with a limp. Wore a long dark jacket. He seemed to familiar I thought I knew him, but when I asked around, no one was certain either."

The storm rattled the windowpanes. She dropped the knife, wiped her hands on her apron, and leaned closer, her eyes sharp. "Carlo's been jumpy ever since you and Enzo mentioned those photographs. And Matteo Rossi's name. For a man who likes to act untouchable, that tells me plenty."

I stared at the half-eaten fig, the honey clinging to my fingers. "Curiosity has a price."

"True," she nodded thoughtfully. "But ignorance costs more. Here take this. At least this won't turn sour on you, unlike half the people in this town," she added, pressing a jar of fig jam into my hands with a wry smile.

Her words landed heavier than I expected. Enzo had been at the lunch at Benedetti's too, had hear the same uneasy words. If anyone could help me make sense of the crate delivery story, it was him. Better to share the news in person than let it grow wild in gossip.

"I'll come," she said, already reaching for her umbrella with a look of resolve. "Two sets of ears hear better than one — and someone has to make sure you don't talk yourself into more trouble, eh!"

The rain had chased away most of the foot traffic in the *piazza*, the gelateria dark and silent under its police seal. I pulled my coat tighter and headed toward the harbor with Lucia. Enzo opened the museum door before we even knocked, relief flashing across his face as though we had spared him the choice of whether to call us.

"I thought you would come," he said, and there was a trace of satisfaction in his voice, as if our arrival confirmed his own unease.

"Because of the crate delivery? You know?" Lucia asked.

Enzo blinked in surprise and nodded. "I saw them unload it from here. Not one of the co-op boats. Hull so old the paint was peeling, no name on the side. They wrestled the old crate straight into the Benedetti's gate door, quick as they could. It struck me as...odd."

He shook his head, frowning. "I don't know what's in it. But after what Vespucci was digging into, it doesn't feel like nothing."

Lucia handed him a fig. "I told you, something's going on."

Enzo rolled the fruit in his palm. "I passed by Benedetti's afterward. The crate was propped at the back entrance, awkward and heavy, as if no one wanted to claim it. Not the kind of thing you expect delivered with the fish and lemons."

My curiosity sharpened. "And?"

"When I went past again later, it wasn't there anymore," Enzo said. "Carlo must have had it moved. If I had to guess, the cellar's the only place he'd keep something like that."

Lucia leaned forward. "Doesn't that sound familiar? Old crates, hidden away where no one should see them..."

Enzo's gaze met mine. "Old stories, like the cannery fire, goods hidden away, never entered in the ledgers. With his reputation, Vespucci wouldn't have been able to resist. If he caught even a hint of that, it might explain why he kept digging."

He shifted against the counter, his shoulder just brushing mine. The closeness wasn't meant for anyone else to notice, not with Lucia standing a step away, but it was enough for me to feel it. She glanced over, then busied herself with the ledger in her hands, as if choosing not to see. I gave a small nod, holding the silence a heartbeat longer than I needed to, the weight of the case pressed up against something more personal that neither of us would name out loud.

Outside, the sound of rain against the shutters, a small reminder of the world waiting beyond the room, pulled us back to the present. We broke apart at the door, agreeing to meet again once the storm passed.

* * *

The wind funneled down the narrow street, rattling the shutters and sending a fine mist of rain under the brim of my hood. I passed the corner by the old pharmacy, where the oleander in its clay planter had been stripped of most of its blossoms. A few pale petals clung stubbornly to the branches, slick with rain, their color muted to almost white in the gloom.

As I made my way home, I couldn't shake the itch between my shoulder blades, the one that told me this wasn't just about Vespucci anymore.

On the way I spotted Maria hurrying across the *piazza*, head down, skirts soaked from the spray. I raised a hand, but she slipped into the trattoria's side door without so much as a glance, as if she hadn't seen me at all.

The rain hammered down by the time I reached my apartment above the old tailor's shop. Water drummed on the awning, the narrow street rushing like a shallow stream. I kicked off my sandals, made tea, and sat by the window, watching as the town blurred into dark watercolors.

And then, through the curtain of rain, I saw him.

The man with the limp.

Suddenly he was real, he was there. He became more than just a shadow in the rain. As he passed beneath the wavering light of a streetlamp, I caught a sharper impression, the uneven hitch in his stride, the way his right shoe dragged half a beat behind the left. A jagged scar curved along his jaw, pale against the coarse stubble, and his hat was tugged low as if to guard against recognition rather than weather.

He clutched a bag tight against his ribs, moving with a practiced wariness that made me certain this wasn't his first time carrying something he didn't want anyone else to see. As he stumbled over a loose cobblestone, his hand slipped, and something white tumbled from his pocket into the streaming gutter.

He didn't notice, too focused on hurrying toward the alley that ran behind Benedetti's.

I was already pulling on my raincoat before my brain caught up. By the time I reached the alley, he was gone, swallowed by the sheets of water and the maze of back streets. Rain still came hard, rattling on bins stacked against the wall, splashing in the deepening puddles.

A white envelope lay sodden in the gutter, its corners softening as the rain gnawed at the paper. I bent to pick it up, pulse thudding harder than it should for a scrap of paper.

My fingers hesitated at the seal. Something about the weight of it — too light to be money, too deliberate to be trash, made my stomach twist. A thousand possibilities spun through my head: a warning, a receipt, proof of whatever game Carlo was playing. For one long second I considered dropping it back into the water and walking away.

But curiosity clawed deeper than fear. I slid my thumb under the soggy flap, the sodden paper parting with a muted rip that seemed louder in my head than the storm outside. Inside, the ink bled slightly from the rain, but the letters still bit through, stark and undeniable:

Crate #47 — 24 bottles. Destination: Benedetti.

Benedetti. Crates. Numbers. It felt all too familiar, like a whisper of something I should already understand. I read the line again, as if repetition would unlock the meaning, but the pieces refused to fit. By the time the storm eased, the words were still burning in my thoughts, refusing to be left behind.

I showed it to Enzo that evening. The rain had eased to a drizzle, and the harbor was quiet except for the creak of mooring ropes.

He smoothed the still slightly wet slip of paper against his knee, careful not to tear it. The ink had blurred in places, but the words were still legible.

"This isn't old," he said. "Looks like a delivery note."

I leaned closer, squinting at the note again, the message remained clear:

Crate #47 — 24 bottles. Destination: Benedetti.

No vineyard name. No distributor stamp. Just a scrawl.

My eye caught on the bottom corner. Two faint initials, half-washed by the rain: *LZ.*

"If it is wine," I asked, "that's not a lot of bottles for a trattoria, why hide where they came from?"

Enzo's mouth tightened. "Because no one wants those bottles traced. It's not how legitimate stock is logged." His gaze flicked toward the trattoria, its windows glowing against the drizzle darkness. "And if Carlo's taking crates like this in the open, with half the town watching, it's no wonder Vespucci started asking questions."

Lucia appeared under her sagging umbrella, dripping like a broken fountain. "Talking about crates again, eh?" she asked with a grin. "Leave that to me."

"Don't tell me you've already got one of your schemes in mind!" I sighed. "Last time you nearly had the postman convinced the mayor was smuggling truffles."

"Hmpf, of course not!" She widened her eyes in mock innocence, then tilted her head as though a thought had just struck her. "Benedetti's niece — Maria, the one who never stops moving? I've seen her serve tables, scrub floors, haul produce from the market before sunrise, all while her uncle shouts orders. Poor thing never smiles." Lucia's lips curved slyly and lifted her finger. "But...she does have a weakness for my candied orange rinds in chocolate. Eh, a bit of chocolate can open the mouth faster than questions ever will."

***

The next day, *Zia* Lucia — efficient as ever when it came to gossip — delivered her report over espresso.

Enzo sat across from me, his cup cooling untouched as he waited for her to get to the point.

"It's wine," she announced. "At least, that's what Maria, the niece, thinks. Carlo told her it was a special vintage from Sicily, a gift from an old friend."

"That's it?" I blurted out, wincing at the disappointment in my own voice.

She gave a little shrug and sipped her coffee. "Maybe. But Maria also said Carlo locked the crate in the cellar and told her not to touch it. Strange, eh? She's the one who usually handles the wine storage."

Enzo leaned back in his chair. "So either it's wine he doesn't want her to see, or it's not wine at all."

I looked between them. "We're making a lot of guesses here."

Lucia smirked. "That's what makes it fun."

But for me, fun wasn't the word. Every step we took toward the truth seemed to open another door, and behind each one was a shadow.

And somewhere in that shadow was the reason Claudio Vespucci had ended up on my shop floor.

That afternoon, Enzo and I returned to the museum. Among the spread of photographs and ledgers, a sheet of thick cream paper caught my eye. Its surface was filled with pleasing precise, looping letters, the kind of handwriting no one teaches anymore. A fountain pen rested beside it, its nib dark with ink.

"Not museum records?" I asked, tilting my head.

Enzo's mouth curved in the faintest smile. "My own indulgence. Calligraphy, old scripts. Copying them keeps my hand steady and my patience intact." He turned the page gently, as though it were centuries old and shrugged. "Some men play cards or go fishing. I spend an evening with ink and silence."

There was something disarming in the admission, in the thought of him bent over pages by lamplight, shaping letters no one else would ever read.

We worked our way through the remaining cannery records. Most of it was dull: delivery slips, maintenance logs. Thankfully Enzo had insisted on asking the archivist about any forgotten boxes, and one had been found and brought up from storage. Among the papers, we came across a photograph tucked inside an envelope marked *Private*.

Enzo drew in a breath, low and sharp. "I knew there had to be more," he murmured, his gaze fixed on the image as if it had been waiting for us all along.

The image showed the inside of the cannery. Matteo Rossi stood with three other men, one of them unmistakably a younger Carlo Benedetti. They weren't posing, just caught mid-movement, hauling wooden crates stenciled with the faint letters *LZ*.

I frowned. "So? Fish in crates — what would Vespucci care?"

Enzo shook his head. "Those aren't fish crates. See the glass symbols, the weight marks? They're for bottles, not sardines. Wine, most likely. And what would wine be doing in a cannery? That's the sort of odd detail Vespucci would notice. He had no problem pressing people with questions, even when they didn't want to answer."

He leaned closer. "The crates — they have the same stenciling as the one delivered to the trattoria last week, I saw it!"

"And look at the calendar on the wall," Enzo continued. "August. Exactly the month the cannery burned. The ledgers survived because they were stored off-site. But this photograph ties Carlo to unmarked shipments right before the fire. To a critic chasing stories, that would have been like striking gold...well, until someone decided he was digging too close."

A chill ran through me. "So Vespucci tripped over a secret that was never meant to see daylight, asking the wrong questions, too loudly."

The thought settled between us, heavy as the humid air.

We left the museum at dusk, the storm lingering like a sulk. Puddles gleamed on the cobbles, and lightning forked far out over the sea, momentarily bleaching the *piazza* in white light. As we were passing Benedetti's, through the trattoria window Carlo's face flickered into clarity with every flash, a man frozen between shadow and lightning. He looked up — and met my gaze. For a heartbeat, neither of us moved. Then he smiled, slow and deliberate, and raised his glass in that slow, mocking toast just as distant thunder broke again, the sound rolled down the street like a warning.

My stomach tightened.

Enzo touched my elbow. "Come on," he murmured.

We walked on, but unease pressed at me. Every step more questions seemed to surface, and someone, somewhere, was already waiting with answers we might not want to hear.

Chapter 7

Shadows on the Cobblestones

Cala d'Oro still sleeps early in May. By ten o'clock, most windows are dark, shutters latched against the sea wind. Off-season quiet suits the locals — they rise early, and with most of the tourists still weeks away, there's little reason to keep the lights burning. The streets empty quickly once the last fishermen have drifted home, only the waterfront bars keep a dim, amber glow, and even those hum quietly, more murmurs than music.

The night was the kind that amplified sound, giving weight to every footfall. And mine weren't the only ones.

I first noticed it as I left Enzo's. His house perched above the harbor, a narrow stone sentinel with green shutters and a cascade of bougainvillea. He met me at the side gate, leading me not back inside, but down to a low outbuilding that smelled of salt, rust, and sun-baked wood.

Under the slanted tin roof, a cherry-red Alfa Romeo slumbered like a relic from a more elegant age. The hood was propped open, a confession of mechanical failure, with wrenches and jars of screws scattered across a bench in organized chaos.

"My other museum," Enzo grinned, wiping his hands on an oily rag. "She ran for glorious twenty minutes last month. Then the carburetor sighed and gave up on me."

I trailed slowly a finger along the flawless curve of the fender. "This doesn't look like frustration. It looks like love...devotion even."

"It's both," he groaned, though his eyes were bright. "Ink stains by morning, grease by night. I have a fondness for broken things." His smile was a quick, private thing. "They keep the mind sharp."

The Alfa was a distraction, a beautiful prelude to the real work. We soon found ourselves back at his desk, the glamour of the car replaced by the gritty reality of more of the old cannery payroll ledgers he located. The pages were soft at the edges, names and wages blurred by decades of humid air. But as we hunched over the columns under the lamplight, a familiar calm settled over me. This was a language I understood. Long before sugar ratios and gelato yields, my life had been measured in spreadsheets and financial statements. While Enzo searched for historical patterns, I found myself instinctively tracing the flow of lira, my old corporate instincts surfacing to spot the subtle discrepancies that others might miss. The dusty ledgers felt like an unexpected homecoming, a reminder that my past held skills that could, it turned out, be just as useful in uncovering the truth as any wrench. This was the real engine we were here to fix.

The main theme: Matteo Rossi's name appeared in places it shouldn't have. Side jobs. "Special deliveries" that were never accounted for in official ledgers. Always in August. One could miss it easily. Always circling the same dates we knew Vespucci had been asking about before he died.

The gentle glow from Enzo's lamp seemed to find every plane of his face, and for a moment, I was more captivated by his focus than the work itself. When his eyes lifted to mine, the look was more than curiosity; it was a silent question, warm and intent, wondering just how far I'd follow him. I knew what my answer was — that I wasn't ready to follow anyone, not even him. But the asking, the unspoken promise I felt, that he might want me to, felt sweet all the same.

The streets were empty when I left. A fine mist slicked the cobblestones, the kind of rain that clings to everything without falling. I headed up Via delle Vele, my bag bumping against my hip with every step toward home.

That's when I heard it, soft, deliberate steps, a few beats behind mine.

At first, I told myself it was nothing. Cala d'Oro's streets are narrow; sound bounces between the walls. But when I stopped to adjust my bag, the footsteps stopped too.

I moved again. So did they.

The prickle at my neck turned into a slow crawl down my spine. I ducked into the alley between the old bakery and the tobacconist's, sandals slapping against slick cobblestones. Halfway down, I risked a glance back.

A shadow detached itself from the darkness and followed. Tall. Thin. A slight hitch in his stride.

The man with the limp.

I quickened my pace, the alley spitting me into a small courtyard. A fountain burbled in the center, its statue of Saint Elmo streaked with lichen. Three exits: the way I'd come, a passage to the *piazza*, and a steep stairwell to the hillside houses.

I took the stairs, pressing into a recessed doorway at the top. His steps came closer, then passed, the limp, or better described as drag, more pronounced on the incline. When I finally stepped out, the street was empty.

I didn't turn on the lights when I reached my flat. I sat in the dark at the kitchen table, watching rain bead on the glass, telling myself my heart rate would slow.

It didn't.

So I stopped waiting for it to. The fear cooled in my veins, hardening into something sharp and usable. I reached for my phone, the screen's blue light cutting through the darkness. I didn't call, didn't text Enzo. Not yet. First, I opened a new note, and my thumbs began to fly, etching every detail into the digital record before the memory could fade: *Tall. Thin. The pronounced drag of the right leg. He knows where I live.*

***

The next morning, a profound quiet had taken root in the Dolce Vita, the kind of silence that only exists in a place normally full of noise and laughter. The chairs were upturned on the tables, and the gelato cases, usually a carnival of color, were dark and empty. It was in this heavy stillness that the realization struck me: I had truly built a life here. I had come to love the messy, sweet chaos of this place, the scent of sugar and espresso, the simple satisfaction of a perfectly swirled cone, the familiar greetings from regulars. This gelateria had become more than a business, it was the center of a world I had chosen, a world I now desperately loved. I moved through the hushed space, the click of my heels on the tile echoing unnaturally, when the door creaked open.

Marco stepped in, nodding toward the CHIUSO sign. "Thought I'd catch you in."

He leaned an elbow on the counter, notepad in hand.

"The lab cleared your gelato. No trace of anything dangerous." Marco ran a hand over his jaw, looking tired. "I called in a few favors, fast-tracked the lab work. Officially, the health inspector could have shut you down for a week or more to be thorough. I kept him off your back."

Relief hit me so hard I had to grip the counter. I could almost hear the bell over the door again, see the line curling again down the street.

"But it's a temporary fix," he added, his tone shifting. "Bianca...he still collapsed here. In people's minds, this will always be where it happened. Until I can give them real answers about how and why, you're not in the clear. And my hands are tied."

The relief thinned to a cold thread. The shop might open its doors again, but until the truth came out, I'd still be running a crime scene.

He pushed off from the counter. "The *Procura* has released the scene. Come on, let's get this eyesore off your door." He walked to the door and, with a precise motion, peeled the end of the yellow police tape from the frame. He wound it into a loose loop, the crinkling sound too loud in the quiet shop. "There. Officially, you're back in business."

"Thank you, Marco. Really."

He gave a short, professional nod, but his eyes held a weight that the simple gesture couldn't lift. He tucked the tape into his pocket and left.

When Lucia arrived later, she took one look at me, then at the bare doorframe where the tape had been. "So. The *carabiniere* has given his blessing."

A tired laugh escaped me. "It's not a blessing, it's procedure. He's the one who sealed it, he's the one who unseals it."

At her puzzled look, I realized the nuance wasn't obvious. "In a town like this? A possible poisoning? By now I learned that's not for the regular police — that's for the *Carabinieri*. They handle the serious stuff. The tape was theirs, the investigation is theirs, so the decision to take it down is theirs. Marco didn't just do me a favor, he was doing his job."

I paused, my voice softening. "He just did it a lot faster than most would have."

Lucia's expression slowly shifted from suspicion to understanding. She gave a slow, appreciative nod. "So, a favor wrapped in a job, eh?"

"Exactly," I shrugged, looking at the clean doorframe. "The right person, doing the right thing, at the right time. He just fast-tracked the lab results so that I could reopen sooner."

"Good." She settled onto a stool, *cornetto* in hand. "But you look like you've either been up all night with a lover or with your thoughts."

"Definitely the second one," I sighed, sliding a coffee across the counter.

"So? What's gnawing at you?"

I told her about the man I'd seen in the rain, the limp, the bag, the envelope. I described his lurching gait and the way he seemed to materialize from the storm.

Lucia's expression shifted from curiosity to dawning recognition, and then darkened. "*Dio mio.* That lurch...you're describing Ettore Rossi. Matteo's younger brother."

I frowned. "Rossi? But if he's so known, why didn't—"

"Because you described a ghost," she cut in, her mouth tightening. "You saw him alone in the rain. Everyone else sees him attached to Carlo Bendetti's hip, hauling crates or lurking by the trattoria's back door. You took away his connection and, eh...without it, he's just a shadow." She let out a short, humorless laugh. "Which I suppose is the point."

"So...he works for Carlo?"

"He comes and goes, spends months on fishing boats down the coast, then drifts back when Carlo needs an extra pair of hands. Or a strong arm. That's why you haven't seen him around." She broke off a piece of *cornetto*. "That limp of his, more of a dragging thing with his left leg, you see it even when he's standing still, it makes folks underestimate him. But don't be fooled. I saw him once chase down a thief who'd stolen from the trattoria. He didn't run, he *lurched*, but fast, like a storm gaining speed! It was more frightening than if he'd been swift and silent. If he was following you, Bianca, it wasn't his own idea. He takes orders. Someone told him to do it."

The name caught me off guard. *Rossi.* My mind snapped back to Marco, standing right where Lucia was sitting, peeling away the police tape. The straight-backed, honorable *carabiniere*. Marco Rossi. Nephew of Matteo Rossi. And now this man, this lurking, dangerous specter with the same name — Ettore Rossi. Matteo's brother and Marco's uncle.

The connection was a live wire. Marco's family wasn't just a respected name in a history book, it had a living, breathing, limping branch that worked for Carlo Benedetti. Vespucci had been poking into the fire, the shipments, the same dates tied to Matteo's name. What if he had been on the verge of connecting dots that would drag the entire Rossi family, past and present, back into disgrace?

Could Marco, desperate to protect his family's name, have slipped something to Vespucci? He'd had every opportunity. The thought made me deeply uneasy. I shook it off. No. The Marco I knew lived by the weight of his badge. But suspicion is a weed, once planted, it doesn't vanish just because you wish it away.

"Carlo's behind this. And Ettore is his instrument." I said finally.

Her voice dropping to barely above a whisper, she leaned closer.

"Listen to me, *cara*. The town talks, I talk, but Carlo Benedetti isn't just talk. Stir up those waters and what rises won't be just rumors. It'll have teeth."

She turned around and shaking her head she added: "Just because you're back in business doesn't mean they've forgotten. They might have your gelato, but they'll still hunger for the truth."

Enzo arrived later mid-morning, the sea breeze ruffling his hair. His sleeves were rolled, showing again intriguing pale scars along his forearms, I resolved to ask him about them one day. He leaned on the counter, eyes steady on mine.

"I heard," he said. "Lucia let me know. About Ettore Rossi, and about Marco's news."

"Of course she did," I muttered, setting finally the cleaning aside.

"She's right, you know...you need to be more careful."

"Bah! I was just walking home," I objected, "not breaking into Carlo's trattoria!"

"And still, Ettore was on your heels," Enzo frowned. "Carlo doesn't send him out for nothing. If he's tailing you, I am sure it means something...they think you've brushed a bit too close to their business."

I folded my arms defiantly. "What business?"

Enzo leaned in, his words barely audible. "I went down to the docks this morning. Found Salvatore and his brother hunched over coffee. They'd spent the night on their trawler, something about the wind and loose moorings. Around two, they heard it: thumping sounds from the far pier, where the shadows run deepest at that hour. The sound of weight being moved in darkness. Come sunrise, nothing remained but salt air and wet footprints. But Salvatore says it's an old tune in Cala d'Oro, played every August like clockwork. Except this year, they're humming it early. May."

A chill of recognition ran through me. "August again."

"Yep. The same month the cannery burned down. The same month those notes about phantom deliveries started being logged in the old records, numbers without goods, shipments no one ever saw." Enzo's gaze was intense. "Now, ask yourself: what is the one business in this town where the right product, arriving off the books, could turn the highest profit? Not fish. Remember what Maria said? She told *Zia* Lucia the other day, without even knowing."

He let the implication hang in the air between us.

"Vespucci was a food critic, but everyone knew wine was his true passion. His palate was legendary. He could taste a story in a glass, and he knew when that story was a lie. What if he wasn't just reviewing Carlo's menu? What if he was reviewing his *cellar*? I think he sensed something that didn't add up. A wine that shouldn't be there. A vintage that spoke of a journey that never happened. His curiosity wouldn't let that rest. He must have started digging and realized Carlo's finest bottles weren't coming through the front door."

I rubbed at my arms, suddenly cold. "And Ettore? Why send him after me? Was it just to scare me off?"

Enzo's expression was grim. "It's a reminder. The whole town knows you're the girl from Milano who untangled that mess for the fashion house. You're not just a *gelataia* to him, you're a forensic consultant who knows how to follow a trail. Carlo doesn't need you asking questions, so he sends a shadow to walk behind you. He doesn't need to hurt you. He just needs you to feel a chill down your spine when you turn a corner, to hesitate before you open your door at night. He wants the fear to do the work for him. It's cheaper, and it's cleaner. As long as you're looking over your shoulder, you're not looking into his business."

The knot in my stomach tightened. It wasn't just my shop or my reputation at stake anymore. Carlo Benedetti was watching me, weighing whether I was a nuisance or a threat.

We moved to a corner table, the daylight pooling between us.

"What's the plan?" I asked.

"We split the work," he said. "You keep digging in the archives. I'll look into this name that keeps surfacing — Lazzaro del Mare."

I tilted my head. "You think it's a person?"

"Could be," Enzo admitted. "Or a front. Sometimes names like that get used to disguise where money or goods are really going. Either way, it shows up too often to be nothing."

"And if I decided to dig into it myself?" I asked, raising a brow.

Enzo leaned back in his chair, the ghost of a smile tugging at his mouth. "I'd tell you to tread lightly. But let's be honest, by now I know you'd nod sweetly and then do the exact opposite."

I tilted my head, pretending to think it over. "So you're saying I'm predictable?"

"Predictable!" he echoed, his grin widening, "Only if you mean in the way a storm is predictable. You know it's coming, you just don't know where it's going to strike."

That earned him a laugh I hadn't realized was sitting in my chest. The heaviness of Lazzaro and crates and shadows loosened for a moment, the air between us easier.

"Do you give this advice to every woman who finds herself tailed by hired muscle, or am I unique?" I teased, leaning in just a little.

Enzo's eyes warmed as they met mine. "Oh, you," he winked, "are absolutely one of a kind."

After Enzo left, I turned the lock and pulled out the box I'd started keeping, my investigation box. Inside were the scraps I gathered so far: photographs, the copied ledger pages from the museum, the envelope I shouldn't still have. My fingers brushed against a slim folder, the collection of photos that represented my greatest risk, and my biggest clue for now.

The memory surfaced, crisp and clear. When Marco dropped in today, he'd waved off my complaint about Ettore incident with a weary sigh — Ettore, he said, was more nuisance than threat, a case already closed. He'd had a stack of folders tucked under his arm, the kind of paperwork he always seemed to carry when the mayor was on his back. He set them on the counter while his phone rang, muttered something about city hall, and stepped outside to take the call.

That was when I saw it, almost hidden among the rest: a slim folder marked in Marco's jagged hand. *Vespucci, C.* was written on the tab.

It was a terrible risk. But Marco's easy dismissal of Ettore had left me cold. He saw a closed case, a nuisance. But I had felt the man's menace, the silent promise it held. If the police weren't going to protect me, if Marco's loyalty to the Rossi family blinded him to the danger one of them posed, then I had to protect myself. The fear of Ettore's shadow was sharper than my conscience. In the several minutes I knew I had, I'd done what I was trained to do in my old life: I'd flipped through, not reading, just scanning for patterns, for anomalies. My phone camera had clicked silently, capturing a dozen pages before the sound of Marco's voice outside the door made me snap the folder shut, every shot hammering a guilty rhythm against my ribs.

Now, in the safety of my empty gelateria, I laid the photos I printed on the counter. Most of it was as

Marco had already mentioned: routine. Train tickets, restaurant bills, reminders scrawled in a restless hand. But then I found it. I had taken a photo of the back of one photograph, the old cannery image I'd also seen at the museum, where in Vespucci's jagged script was penciled a single word, underlined twice:

Lazzaro.

I turned the photo over again and again, as if the answer might appear in the grain of the paper. A name, a place, a signature? This was it. This was the word repeated in the old records, a proof that Marco's 'routine' file contained something he had either missed or intentionally ignored. My gelateria might have been cleared by official decree, but this word, this secret buried in a detective's notes, carried a meaning I was sure. Somehow, it felt heavier than everything else in the box, as though Vespucci had really circled closer to something vital, and his discovery had been neatly filed away and forgotten.

Later, when I stepped onto my balcony, the sea shimmered silver in the moonlight. Cala d'Oro looked perfectly peaceful, like a painted postcard. But fairy tales always look harmless, until you remember there's always someone lurking in the shadows.

And the most dangerous secrets weren't only in Benedetti's circles. They were in a police folder I shouldn't have photos of, and in the Rossi family, with Marco standing guard over more than just the law. And I was certain the man with a limp, Ettore Rossi, was still out there, watching, making the peaceful town below feel like a gilded cage. A cage I now knew I had to pick the lock on myself.

Chapter 8

Shifting Ground

The bell above Dolce Vita's door didn't ring so much as sigh, a hollow sound that emphasized the silence it failed to break. Morning light streamed in, too cheerful for the grim atmosphere. I'd opened early out of habit, but the habit felt hollow. The espresso machine hissed and steamed, a performance for an audience of one. Marco had cleared my name, but the town's memory was longer than any official report. They remembered the scandal, not the exoneration. The air itself carried a stubborn aftertaste of doubt.

The door opened and *Zia* Lucia slipped in, a splash of color in a lemon-yellow scarf and oversized sunglasses. She pulled them off, her sharp eyes missing nothing.

"You look like you've been arguing with your own shadow, eh?" she said, sliding onto a stool.

"And losing," I admitted, handing a cappuccino across to her.

She took a sip, her gaze sweeping the empty shop. "Polishing glass again?"

"No, no, it's clean," I said, though the rag in my hand betrayed me.

"Yes, I can see that, but can you?" she asked, her voice dripping with sarcasm. She set her cup down with a definitive click. "You can't hide behind this counter forever, Bianca. Carlo won't wait, and neither will the truth."

I leaned forward, lowering my voice. "I keep thinking about last night. About Ettore. What if letting him pass was a mistake? What if that was my one chance to see what he's carrying for Carlo?"

Lucia's expression turned stern. "Ettore Rossi is not a man you follow. He is a man you thank God didn't stop." She saw the unspoken question in my eyes. "And don't start on Marco. His father nearly broke his back pulling that boy out of his uncle's shadow. Don't go planting weeds where there's no garden."

"So I'm imagining things?"

"I'm saying suspicion is like salt water," she replied. "A little keeps you afloat. Too much, and you drown."

After she left, the silence felt even heavier. I wiped down the already-spotless counter, the motion futile. My phone buzzed, shattering the quiet.

Enzo. At the museum. Come by. Found something.

The message was a lifeline. I didn't bother with a note. I flipped the sign to CHIUSO, a lie for anyone who might finally dare to come in, and left.

I found him outside the museum, a canvas bag slung over his shoulder, a look of focused energy on his face. "I found Lazzaro," he said without preamble.

"Already? So is it a person?"

"Sort of." He gestured toward the harbor, and we fell into step. "There's no 'Lazzaro' in any recent records. But in the museum's oral histories, old fishermen mention a *Lazzaro del Mare* — the 'Lazarus of the Sea.' It's not a person. It's the old boathouse beyond Punta Seca."

"What? Why call a boathouse Lazarus?"

"Because it keeps coming back as I understood," he frowned. "Storms knocked it down twice in the seventies. They rebuilt it both times with cannery timber. People said it wouldn't stay dead."

The penciled name on the back of the photograph suddenly made terrifying sense. "Ah! So it's a place. A stash point maybe?"

"Exactly. If you're moving crates you tell people are wine, you'd use a half-forgotten relic off the main quay." He tapped his folder. "Now let's see if *Zia* Lucia remembers the details. If anyone might know whether Lazzaro was ever more than a name, it will be her.""

We walked through the streets rinsed clean by the storm, the air sharp with salt and wet stone. The market was still shaking itself awake, vendors tugging at tarps, calling out prices, gulls wheeling overhead.

As we turned past the fish market, a familiar voice called our names. Lucia was perched on a low stone wall, after leaving my shop clearly intent on enjoying the morning sun.

She held a small *pasticceria* bag and was dusting powdered sugar from her fingers. She waved us over. "There you are," she said, standing up. "When Enzo calls and says 'I need your memory,' a woman comes. Especially for Lazzaro del Mare." She gestured with the bag. "I brought a *sfogliatella* for you. The *cannoli* were already gone, the vultures."

Enzo smiled and got straight to the point. "The records say the name, but not what it was used for."

A shadow of old caution crossed Lucia's face. "Lazzaro del Mare," she repeated, the name a secret on her tongue. "You don't hear that anymore. It's just the old boathouse, crumbling into the sea now. My father said that place was where the sea kept its secrets. Teenagers went to misbehave. Others? For things that wouldn't bear the sunlight. Crates that came in on the tide and left before dawn. We all knew to look the other way."

Looking from Enzo to me, her gaze sharpened as she understood his intent. "So that's why you called for my memory. You're not just asking about stories, you're thinking of going down there, eh?"

Straightening up, her mind was made up. "And no, I am not waving goodbye. Your Nonna would rise and scold me. The path is narrow. The planks rot. Keep to the stone. Watch the swell. If the tide pushes, you turn back. I'll wait by the fig tree. If you're not back in couple of hours, I go to Marco. No arguments."

"Thank you, Lucia," I said, a knot of gratitude tightening in my chest.

"Someone has to keep you from walking straight into the sea," she said, pointing a finger at me before turning to Enzo. "Make sure she comes back in one piece."

"I'm just trying to keep up with her," he replied, a flicker of amusement in his eyes.

***

As we started down the path, I glanced back. A sensible person would bring Marco. But sense warred with suspicion. What if he was still his uncle's nephew? We needed to see for ourselves first.

Beyond the bluffs, the town fell away. The air smelled of sun-warmed kelp and tar. There, hunched against the rocks like a sullen old man, was the boathouse: weather-gray planks, a mismatched tile roof, patched with corrugated tin, one door and one window dark as shut eyes.

“Charming,” I commented, though my voice caught on the word.

“Wait until you meet the resident spiders,” Enzo murmured, too lightly, as if humor could smooth the tension in the air.

Up close, the neglect looked deliberate: a new padlock, fresh rope on a rusted hook, boot prints in the sand that hadn’t blurred.

“Someone’s been here. Recently,” I pointed to the foot marks.

“Or last night.” Enzo crouched, examining the sand with the absorption of a man who’s always finding stories in fragments. “Two sets of prints. One normal stride. One with a...hitch.”

My mouth went dry. “The limp. Ettore was here.”

He nodded once. Then he straightened, scanned the horizon, reached into his bag and handed me a pair of thin cotton gloves.

“I thought we were just looking,” I noted drily, pulling the gloves on.

“We are. Carefully.”

The padlock looked robust until Enzo prodded it with his thumbnail and it swung on a screw that hadn't been tightened fully. Not real security, stage dressing. My heartbeat climbed another step as he eased the hook free and shouldered the door.

The smell hit first: brine and old wood, oil and distant rot. The interior was one long room with racks for oars, a low beam that would scalp anyone over six feet, and dust that swirled in light from the single window. A dinghy lay belly-up on blocks. In the far corner, stacked like props waiting for their cue, were three wooden crates banded in tarnished steel. Weathered. Familiar.

"Just like the photo," I whispered.

"Exactly." Enzo crossed to the nearest crate, brushing grime from a knot in the wood. A faint black stamp appeared: LZ-51.

My skin prickled. I ran my fingers along a damp beam, tracing rough, deliberate letters gouged into the wood: LZ. The same initials from the chit Ettore had dropped. A signature.

Enzo pressed his ear to the crate lid, then rapped it with his knuckles. "Solid, but not quite." His fingers slid along the seam, probing. "Here..." he murmured. Beneath the layer of grime his thumb found a recessed catch. With a quick twist it clicked, releasing a concealed latch.

Inside, straw was packed thick. He pulled out a bottle — Sicilian, 1997, cork sealed with red wax.

"Wine," I breathed, feeling both disappointed and relieved. "Of course, it's wine!"

"Maybe," he replied, examining the bottle. "Or maybe it's something else, considering how the crate was secured," he said, digging deeper until his knife hit wood. A false bottom. He pried it open.

Enzo was right. Inside lay a slim oilskin notebook, a packet of photos bound with ribbon, and a damp-softened envelope.

The photos were ghosts from the past: men in the cannery, crates stacked high; a night shot of the harbor; a candid of a young, lean Carlo and Matteo Rossi grinning like he owned the future.

Enzo's voice was low. "The notebook. Dated entries from 1990. Initials. B for Benedetti. M.R. for Matteo Rossi. And a 'C.' — an outside contact." He flipped to the back, easing out a train ticket stub. Ravenna to Cala d'Oro. August 16. The day after the fire.

My hands trembled as I opened the envelope. The handwriting was cramped, but clear.

August 12. First shipment received at Lazzaro. B. insists on cash only.

August 14. Meeting with Benedetti. M.R. to handle transfers. M.R. off roster. Asking questions. Move plates off-site.

August 15. Margin note: M.R. says he will burn it. Cannery stock written off.

August 16. Ravenna contact C. to confirm payment.

"The cannery was a cover," I said, the words hollowing my chest. "Matteo was one of them. He handled it. But then he's 'off roster.' 'Asking questions.' A falling out? We will never know..."

"...and his solution was to burn it all down?" Enzo asked quietly noone in particular, tapping the margin note. "Perhaps. To hurt Carlo, or wipe the slate clean. He just never meant to be inside when it happened."

He closed the notebook carefully. "This wasn't left here by accident. This was insurance. A threat. Something that could ruin these men even twenty years later."

A faint scrape echoed from outside. We froze. A footfall. Slow, dragging. Another.

Enzo's gaze flicked to mine, steady as stone, before he slid the bundle back into its canvas wrap. He pressed it into my hands, pointed to the dinghy, and raised a finger to his lips.

I crouched and slid the package into the hollow beneath the stern, tucking it under the loose plank we'd noticed earlier. Enzo reset the board with practiced ease, scattering a bit of sand and straw over the seam until it looked untouched. Then he returned to the crates, smoothed the false bottom into place, settled a bottle back on top, and pressed the lid down until the nails sat flush again and ran to the dinghy, which became our hiding place.

By the time the door creaked wider, the boathouse looked as bare and abandoned as when we had first stepped inside.

The man entered with the weather, carrying the smell of sweaty cloth and the acrid tang of cheap tobacco. His shape filled the doorway — tall, angular, shoulders sloped from years of work. Each step carried that faint drag: left foot trailing, leather scraping wood.

He paused just inside, letting the light adjust, then crossed to the stacked crates. For a moment he only stood there, head cocked, listening, as if the wood itself might whisper its secrets. Then he crouched, ran a long finger along the seam of the lid we had so carefully reset, and inhaled, sharp and deliberate.

My pulse thundered in my throat.

He rose and walked to the window, pausing to gaze at the sea glinting like polished metal, before warily surveying the room. When he came near our hideout, close enough that I noticed the worn-down heel of his shoe and a rust-colored mark on his sleeve, my lungs seized, a reflex beyond my control.

He reached up suddenly and yanked a coil of rope from a peg. It fell to the floor with a slap that echoed off the planks. I flinched. Enzo's hand found my wrist and squeezed with a small, grounding pressure.

The man coiled the rope lazily now, like he'd only come for that, then he slung it over his shoulder and left, the door groaning behind him. Footsteps receded. A gull laughed. Somewhere a boat knocked against its mooring.

We didn't move for a count of thirty.

"My least favorite field trip ever," I finally whispered.

"We're not done." Enzo said while peering out the door. "He's heading back. We'll take the low route along the rocks, circle back, and see where he goes."

We scrambled over slick stones, the sea soaking our ankles, and cut inland, emerging on a lane above the harbor just as Ettore reached the town's edge.

He moved with purpose, ducking into the alley behind Benedetti's and slipping through a narrow back gate inside.

"Of course, where else!" I grumbled under my breath.

"Shhh, stay focused," Enzo hissed.

From a hidden nearby bench, we watched the courtyard. Ettore reappeared with an empty basket, knocked a pattern on the door — two, one, two — and slipped inside. A pale, younger hand held the latch. Not Carlo's.

Minutes later, he emerged, basket now full, tucking a folded paper into his pocket. At the gate, he paused, his head cocked, his eyes scanning the alley with a new, sharp wariness.

"He's on alert," Enzo breathed. "Checking his tail. We can't follow him now."

I started to rise. "Then the back door —"

"— is a trap waiting for you," he finished, his hand on my arm. "Carlo already knows we're circling. Ettore followed you to rattle you. Walking in there isn't just risky, it's stepping into the lion's den."

"This isn't a hobby, Enzo! It's survival. If Carlo killed Vespucci for getting too close, then proving it is the only way I get my life back!"

His expression softened but his resolve didn't. "Then we walk in together. We let him talk. We watch. Every word, every glance. If he made a mistake once, he'll make another."

I nodded, my resolve hardening like cooled sugar. "Good. Because I have no intention of being remembered as the woman who killed a critic with gelato."

A faint smile touched his lips. "Let's make sure you're remembered for something else, then."

Chapter 9

Key to the Past

The morning after the boathouse, the air on the quay felt different, charged with a new and perilous gravity. It was still sharp with the tang of salt and the piercing cries of the gulls wheeling overhead, but the postcard perfection of Cala d'Oro now seemed like a thin, flaking veneer over something rotten festering beneath. The brightly painted fishing boats, bobbing gently in the harbour, looked like props. The joyful shouts of the fishermen unloading their catch sounded staged and distant. I found Enzo leaning against a rusted iron capstan, its ancient mechanism seized by time and salt.

His gaze was not on the picturesque harbour, but fixed on the industrial horizon beyond, where the active quay gave way to a row of old, salt-bleached storage sheds, their windows boarded up, their doors sagging on corroded hinges. He looked like he hadn't slept, the lines around his eyes etched deeper than usual, his shoulders set with a tension that was more than just physical fatigue.

"You look like I feel," I said, coming to stand beside him, my own sleepless night a heavy weight behind my eyes.

He didn't turn immediately, his attention still captured by the derelict sheds. "I've been thinking," he said finally, his voice low and gravelly from the night air and lack of rest. "All night, I've been turning it over. Watching Ettore deliver something to Carlo's back door changes nothing in the eyes of the law, just a story we tell. We have some old photos and a cryptic notebook from a crumbling shack that could have been written by anyone. It's all history, Bianca. A ghost story. To shake a man like Carlo Benedetti from his throne, we need something current. Something concrete and undeniable that ties the past in that boathouse directly to him as of today."

I couldn't keep the skepticism from my voice. "And how do you propose we get that? Walk up to his door and ask for a tour? Present him with a questionnaire?"

He turned to me then, and a strange, determined light flickered in his eyes, a look that was both thrilling and terrifying. "In a manner of speaking. We're going for a coffee."

I stared at him, waiting for the punchline, for the wry smile that would signal a dark joke. It didn't come. His expression remained deadly serious. "You have lost your mind!" I stated, the words leaving my lips before I could stop them. "We just agreed last night that Carlo's den is a lion's trap. We walk in there, and he'll know why we've come."

"We're not going to kick the door down. We're not going to accuse him," he said, his voice dropping lower, forcing me to lean in. "We're going to be perfectly normal, curious, slightly rattled citizens. The town is still buzzing with the news of Vespucci's death anyways. And while we're there, while I keep him occupied, you're going to find a way into the cellar."

A laugh, sharp and incredulous, escaped me. It was a brittle sound that was quickly carried away by the wind. "How, Enzo? Do you have a blueprint tucked away in that historian's brain of yours? A secret password? Should I just pick the lock with a hairpin?"

A faint, almost smug smile touched his lips, the first sign of the man I now knew better, breaking through the grim facade. He reached into his worn canvas messenger bag, the one that always smelled of old paper and leather, and rummaged for a moment before pulling out a small, lumpy object. It was a worn leather pouch, darkened with age and soft from use. He loosened the drawstring with deliberate slowness and tipped its contents into his palm.

A single, flat brass key on a frayed red string lay against his skin, gleaming dully in the morning light.

I fell silent, all my sarcasm evaporating into the salt-heavy air. My eyes were locked on the unassuming object. “What is that?” I breathed, though some part of me already knew.

“This,” he said, holding it up between his thumb and forefinger so it caught the weak morning sun, “is a piece of local history. And it might just be the one thing that fits Carlo Benedetti’s cellar door.”

My mind raced, trying to connect the dots between a museum historian and the door in a local trattoria. “Enzo,” I said, my voice hushed with a mixture of hope and alarm, “how on earth could you possibly have a key to Carlo Benedetti’s trattoria cellar? Did you steal it?”

“I don’t have *his* key,” he corrected, his tone shifting into the familiar, patient rhythm of the historian lecturing a fascinated student. It was a comforting cadence, utterly at odds with the fraught subject matter. “I have *a* key. You have to understand, Carlo’s father, Alberto Benedetti, was a notoriously cheap and uhm…pragmatic man, Bianca. When he renovated the trattoria twenty-odd years ago, he scavenged every usable material from the cannery demolition site. He didn’t see history, he just saw free hardware, reusable fixtures.”

He tapped the key with his finger. "These locks, the original, heavy iron ones on the cellar and the rear doors, they weren't from the main cannery building that burned in the '90s. That would have been impossible as they were melted to scrap. These were salvaged from a storage shed just on the perimeter, a smaller brick building the fire barely licked. Solid, old-world craftsmanship, built to last a century. Why buy new, flimsy locks when these formidable ones were just sitting there, waiting for a new purpose?"

The sheer, audacious simplicity of it left me temporarily speechless. It was a gamble founded on a miser's character flaw. "And the museum...?" I prompted, the pieces clicking slowly into place.

"...has the master set for all the cannery's original outbuildings," he finished, a note of triumph in his voice. "Donated years ago when we did the 'Cala d'Oro at Work' exhibit. Carlo's father saw a bargain. He never considered it a security risk. To him, it was just a lock. He never imagined someone would care years later." He reached out and pressed the key into my hand. The metal was cool, its edges worn smooth from age and use. "It might not work. Carlo might have changed the locks when he took over. He's more modern, more paranoid. But if he's as arrogant and frugal as his father was...if he saw replacing a perfectly good, solid lock as a pointless expense...well, it just might fit."

I closed my fingers around it. It felt impossibly light for the immense weight of the risk it represented. This wasn't just a key, it was a gamble on a dead man's thrift, a bet placed with our lives as the wager.

"So the plan is to walk into the lion's den," I said, my voice barely a whisper, almost swallowed by the lap of water against the quay. "You provide the distraction, the conversation. And I...I just slip away like a ghost and try this old key in a door that could lead to the one place I should never, ever be. The place where he keeps his secrets."

"Yes," he said, his gaze unwavering, solid as the stone of the quay itself. "That's the plan."

I looked from the key in my hand to his serious, tired face. The cost of failure was very likely the end of everything — my freedom, my home I built in Cala d'Oro, any hope of justice for Vespucci. The cost of inaction, of letting Carlo win, was the same — a lifetime of living under his shadow, in a town forever poisoned by his corruption. The calculation was terrifyingly simple, a binary choice between two terrible outcomes.

I took a deep breath, the cold, clean salt air filling my lungs one last time before we stepped into the stifling atmosphere of the trattoria. “Okay.”

He nodded once, a look of fierce, grim pride flashing in his eyes. He didn’t offer empty platitudes or false reassurance. He simply acknowledged the step we were taking, together. “Okay.”

Several minutes later, after a silent, nerve-wracking walk through the waking town, we were walking through the alternating bars of shadow and light cast by Benedetti’s striped awning. The trattoria, usually a place of warmth and gossip, now felt like a meticulously constructed stage set, every clink of cutlery too loud, every glance from the few early patrons too long and knowing. Carlo stood behind the bar, a storm cloud contained in a spotless white apron, polishing a wine glass with a slow, deliberateness that felt like a silent threat. His smile, when it slowly found us, was a cold event, not reaching his eyes.

“Bianca. *Signor* Valli.” His words were slick, like oil on water, meant to smooth over any ripples of discord. “Back so soon? After the...unpleasantness? I’m flattered you consider my establishment a refuge.”

I summoned a smile from some deep, untapped well of courage, hoping it didn’t look as brittle and fragile as it felt. "The gelateria's cleared," I said, forcing a lightness into my tone I didn't feel, "but there's no point pretending business is normal when everyone's still whispering about poor Claudio Vespucci. Better to step back for a bit, let the dust settle, until I can find a way to clear my name."

He set the glass down on the polished mahogany bar. The *click* it made was definitive, a full stop to the conversation. "Everyone wants to clear their name when tongues start wagging," he said, his eyes holding mine, as if probing for weakness. "But in my experience, *Signorina* Moretti, digging too hard into ugly rumors only gives them new life, new soil to grow in. Some weeds are best left unpulled. Better to let some things lie."

The warning was velvet-covered steel. I forced myself to meet his gaze, to not let my eyes flicker away in fear. "Maybe," I conceded, neither agreeing nor disagreeing, leaving him guessing.

We took a small table for two near the kitchen's swinging door — a strategic choice that offered a view of the entire room and a potential escape route. Enzo ordered two espressos and some *cantucci*, the perfect props for our performance of two locals taking a quiet break. I felt utterly exposed, my panic a palpable force in the air between us. I was certain Carlo must feel it across the room.

I could see straight down the back hallway from where I sat. Carlo's niece, Maria, emerged carrying a tray, her movements quick and efficient despite her youth. When she spotted us, her hands faltered for just a heartbeat, the slightest tremor that nearly sent a spoon sliding, before she composed herself with practiced speed. Flicker crossed Enzo's face. Nothing escaped him either.

The key in my dress pocket felt like a brand, a searing point of focus. I was hyper-aware of everything: the way Maria now carefully and deliberately avoided making eye contact as she wiped down tables, the too-loud, oblivious laughter from a table of French tourists studying a map, the constant, watchful presence of Carlo himself, a predator pretending to be a host, polishing glasses that already shone.

Then, salvation and terror intertwined. His mobile phone buzzed on the bar with an insistent vibration. He scowled at the screen, then picked it up. He turned his back to the room, his free hand cupping his ear, his voice dropping to a low, intent murmur. The trattoria's noise, the chatter, the clattering from the kitchen, it all seemed to dip at that exact, providential moment, funneling few crystal-clear words across the room to our table.

"...no more delays. The...the material in my cellar, it all goes by end of the week. Tutto. *No mistakes. And remember to prepare the boat, make it look like a routine run. Understood?"*

Unease tightened in my chest. My hand, resting on the table, trembled slightly, and I quickly placed my other over it to still it. He'd just given us the timeline. He wasn't just hiding evidence I was sure. He was moving it, maybe destroying it. By end of the week. We had a few days only. It wasn't just now or never. It was *now*.

I looked at Enzo. His jaw was tight, a muscle flickering in his cheek. His face was grim, all traces of the historian gone, replaced by the resolve of a man who knows the moment of action has arrived. He gave me a nearly imperceptible nod, his eyes darting towards the dark corridor that led to the restrooms.

"Count to ten," he murmured under his breath, picking up his water glass and not looking at me. "The bathroom is down the corridor on the left, you know. The cellar door next to it, at the very end. It's our only chance."

My fingers found the key in my pocket, the cool brass now warmed by my skin. I took a steadying breath, mentally counting, each number a hammer blow in my chest. One. Two. Three.

I rose, smoothing my dress with clammy palms, and slung my purse over my shoulder with a studied casualness. "I'll be right back," I said, my voice miraculously steady, a minor win in the face of the vertigo threatening to overwhelm me.

I didn't look at Carlo. I didn't look back at Enzo. I walked toward the dim hallway, each step feeling like a mile, the merry sounds of the trattoria fading behind me as if I were descending into a well. There was no going back now. The lion's den, and its deepest, darkest secret, lay ahead.

Chapter 10

Where the Light Fell

The hallway was a throat, narrow and dark, swallowing the buoyant noise of the trattoria behind me. The air here was different, a cloying mix of lemon-scented polish and the underlying, stale grease of decades of cooking. It felt heavy, oppressive. At the far end stood the cellar door, solid, imposing, and freshly painted a glossy white that seemed to repel the dim light. Next to it, the bathroom door stood slightly ajar, a sliver of white tile visible.

Dread washed over me, raising gooseflesh on my skin, a betrayal in the tomblike silence of the passage. Every instinct screamed at me to turn back, to retreat to the relative safety of the dining room and its illusion of normalcy. But the image of the key in my pocket, and the memory of Carlo's voice on the phone — *the material in my cellar* — propelled me forward.

I nudged the bathroom door wider. My eyes scanned the *bagno*, not for its purpose, but for its potential. And there it was. An idea, desperate and brilliant, sparked in my mind. The key was in the lock on the inside. If I could lock this door from the outside, it would buy me precious time, create an alibi. I slid the key out, its metal icy against my sweating palm. I pulled the door shut from the hallway, my movements furtive and quick, and turned the key. The mechanism clicked with a sound that seemed deafening in the hush. *Occupied.* A simple, universal signal. If anyone tried the handle, they'd assume I was still inside, and the locked door would be a barrier, a reason for anyone to leave.

Pocketing the bathroom key, a new weight alongside the brass one, I turned to face the cellar door. This was it. My mouth was dry, my breath shallow.

I pulled the brass key from my pocket, the piece of local history, the testament to a cheap man's arrogance, the gamble of a lifetime. My hand trembled slightly as I guided it toward the lock. I half-expected it to not fit, for the plan to crumble here on the threshold, saving me from the danger beyond.

It slid in. Smoothly. Perfectly.

Turning it, the motion feeling impossibly loud. The mechanism, old, but in good shape, gave way with a soft, well-oiled *click* that was in reality almost silent. A shudder of mingled triumph and terror went through me. Carlo's confidence was his greatest flaw, he'd never imagined anyone would be both daring enough and equipped with the right part of the past to dare. His father's thrift had built a backdoor into his son's empire.

I counted to three, each number a thud in the silence, then grasped the cool iron handle. I pulled. The door groaned on its hinges, a low, protesting sound that seemed to vibrate through the floorboards and echo through the entire building. A wave of cool, humid air washed over me, smelling of rich earth, old cork, and faintly of forgotten wood. Without another second's hesitation, I slipped inside, pulling the door shut behind me, the latch sealing me into the profound darkness of Carlo Benedetti's secrets.

For a moment, I was blind, my other senses screaming in the void. The air was still and cold. I fumbled for my phone, swiped it on, and used the dim light of the screen to orient myself. A steep, narrow flight of wooden steps descended into the gloom. I descended them lightly, my soft-soled shoes making little sound, counting them as I went, five down, a small landing where the stairs turned, then four more. The wood creaked under my weight, each sound a potential betrayal.

At the bottom, the cellar unfolded before the weak light of my phone. It was a low-ceilinged, brick-lined room, larger than I'd imagined, lined with racks and stacks of crates. The beams overhead were thick, rough-hewn wood, and cobwebs draped the corners like dusty lace.

Moving swiftly, my eyes adjusting, using the phone's light like a torch. The racks closest to the stairs held what you'd expect: cases of house Chianti, sturdy Nero d'Avola, boxes of olive oil. Then my gaze snagged on a separate, more carefully arranged section. The labels here were different. My body went rigid. Château Lafite Rothschild. Domaine de la Romanée-Conti. Sassicaia. Bottles like these, vintages this old, didn't just sit in any trattoria cellar, they were priceless trophies fought over at auctions, some surely kept in climate-controlled vaults. My own curiosity overrode my fear. I reached out and picked up a bottle of '89 Lafite. It felt wrong. Too light. I gave it a gentle, experimental shake. No liquid sloshed inside. It was empty. A decoy. A beautiful, expensive-looking prop. My mind raced. Were they for display? To impress certain guests? Or were they part of something else entirely?

A sudden rush filled my ears. I turned from the wine racks, sweeping my phone's light toward the far corner, behind a stack of empty vegetable crates. And there they were. A neat stack of six wooden crates, darker and older than the others, stamped with faded but familiar black marks: LZ-47, LZ-48, LZ-53. The same markings from the boathouse ledger. The same markings on the crate Ettore had delivered.

This must be it. The core of it.

I crouched beside them, the damp from the dirt floor seeping through my dress. My fingertips ran along the rough slats, feeling the grain of the wood. At the boathouse, Enzo had shown me how to feel for seams that didn't belong, for panels that were meant to move. I tried the same here, pressing and probing on the sides and bottom of the third crate. One side felt solid. The other did not. I pressed harder on the bottom edge. It yielded with a soft, almost inaudible *crack*, a cleverly designed latch giving way. No tools required. It was meant to be accessed quickly, discreetly.

Holding my breath, I pried it open, the wood rasping softly against itself. Beneath a shallow layer of straw packing and a few token, legitimate-looking bottles of wine, the same decoys as upstairs, something else was tucked away. A long, heavy canvas wrap, like a tool roll. My hands were shaking now, from the adrenaline. I slid it free, the weight of it surprising me. It felt like metal. I unrolled it carefully across the top of the open crate.

Steel glinted in the faint light of my phone. Not books, not rusted tools. Molds — hefty, precision-cut plates of steel, meticulously engraved with the intricate seals and crests of the very French and Italian wineries. Beside them, nestled in separate pockets of the roll, lay a compact, professional-looking hand-press with interchangeable typefaces and stacks of heavy, high-quality, embossed paper, pre-printed with the headers of renowned auction houses, certificates of authenticity and provenance documents.

I realized with astonishment: this was a portable, perfect forgery kit. Everything a master counterfeiter needed to turn cheap plonk into a collector's prize worth thousands, bottles that are almost never opened, just owned.

The full, sickening scope of it hit me. This wasn't mere evidence, it was a glimpse into the engine room of the crime itself, with the main controls likely far from here. Enzo guessed it. The cannery had been the perfect cover in the past, shipments of fish in, crates of "wine" out, odd numbers blurred in the ledgers until no one could tell what was real.

And when they turned on each other, threatening exposure, the fire had burned it all clean. And Vespucci. He must have found one of Carlo's so called "rare vintages" wanting. A food critic and wine connoisseur lived on details — acidity, bouquet, and especially provenance. He would have checked the certificates, suspected something, and pulled the wrong thread. He hadn't needed rumors. He'd stumbled onto some form of proof.

And it had cost him his life.

Carlo wasn't just a surly restaurateur with questionable wine. He was a counterfeiter willing to silence anyone who threatened his operation. And I'd just become possibly the second person to discover his secret.

I fumbled for my phone, my fingers suddenly clumsy and numb. I thumbed the camera app open, my hand shaking so badly I almost dropped the device. The flash. It would be a beacon in the dark, a flare announcing my presence. I held my breath, listening so intently the blood roared in my ears. Nothing. Silence. I had to risk it. I pressed the button.

The flash exploded, a starburst of blinding white light that illuminated every dust mote, every cobweb, the damning archive of his crime in stark, shocking detail. I flinched at the noise it seemed to make. I took picture after picture, moving quickly around the crate, capturing the molds, the press, the papers from every angle, my heart hammering against my ribs, a silent prayer on repeat in my mind: *don't let him see, don't let him hear, don't let that sliver of light under the door have just signed my death warrant.*

I had just taken the last photo, my finger hovering over the button to check them, when I heard it.

A floorboard creaked directly overhead. A heavy footstep. Then another. Muffled voices. Someone was in the corridor.

Now. Panic, numbing and sharp, injected itself into my veins. I moved fast, my actions becoming frantic. I rewrapped the heavy molds, my fingers fumbling with the canvas, and slid the bundle back into its hiding place. I reset the false bottom, pressing until I heard the soft sound of the latch engaging. I closed the lid, smoothing the straw back into place, trying to make it look undisturbed. I was halfway up the stairs, taking them two at a time, when the door next to the cellar, the bathroom door, rattled.

Someone was trying the handle.

"*Occupato*!" I called out, layering my voice with cheerful, slightly annoyed embarrassment. It didn't sound like me, it sounded like a stranger, a woman irritated at being interrupted.

Silence from the other side of the door. Then a muffled, male apology, and the sound of retreating footsteps. A ragged sigh escaped me as the unconscious tension finally broke. I climbed the rest of the way, the brass key already in my hand.

I cracked the cellar door open a fraction, listening. The hallway was empty. Or so I thought. From the deep shadows of a recessed service doorway further down the hall, I noticed a pair of wide, frightened eyes watched me. Maria must have noticed the flash of light under the cellar door. But in this moment, she didn't cry out. She didn't alert her uncle. She simply pressed herself deeper into the shadows, holding her breath, understanding in a flash that I, too, was an enemy of Carlo Benedetti. She nodded and quietly watched me slip out, lock the cellar door with a key that shouldn't exist, and then unlock the bathroom I was supposedly occupying to start with. And in that shared, silent understanding, a fragile thread of trust was spun between us.

After I was back in the *bagno,* I turned on the tap full blast, the water roaring in the small room, and splashed fresh water on my face, trying to shock the panic from my features. I looked at myself in the mirror. My eyes were wide, my skin pale. I looked guilty. I took several deep, steadying breaths, ran my fingers through my hair as if battling the humidity, and practiced a neutral expression. *Normal. You are just a woman who used the bathroom.*

When I emerged, trying to seem slightly bored, the hallway was still empty. I walked back to the dining room, every step feeling like I was walking through glue. Enzo's expression didn't shift, his face a masterclass in neutral observation, but I saw the minute release of tension in his jaw, the almost imperceptible relaxation of his shoulders. He'd been holding his breath the entire time.

Carlo appeared almost immediately, as if summoned by my return, carrying a small silver tray with two tiny porcelain espresso cups. Not his niece, not a waiter. *Him.* The man whose secret I had just violated, whose criminal enterprise I had just documented, was serving me coffee. The surreal horror of it made my pulse rattle against my bones.

"Your espresso," he said lightly, setting the cups down with a deliberate, almost ceremonial care. "Strong enough to wake the dead, no?" His eyes flicked up to meet mine, and for a terrifying second, I thought I saw a glint of knowing amusement in their depths.

His hand brushed mine as he withdrew. It was a fleeting, accidental touch, cold from holding the tray, but every nerve in me flared as if he'd pressed a brand straight into my skin. *I know,* the touch seemed to whisper. *I know what you did.*

I forced my hand to be steady, to lift the tiny cup. The coffee's intense bitterness curled into the back of my throat, but the taste that stayed on my tongue, coating it, was the pure, metallic flavor of fear.

"Delicious," I said, careful to make my voice sound steady, normal, utterly unaware.

"'Unforgettable,'" Enzo followed, his tone dry and academic, giving away nothing, as if commenting on the blend.

Carlo's smile twitched, a small, dangerous movement at the corner of his mouth, then smoothed again into a bland, professional mask. He gave a faint, almost regal nod and drifted back to his post behind the bar, picking up a spotless glass and beginning to polish it anew, his gaze returning to us like the tide, steady, patient, inescapable.

We didn't linger. We paid with cash, the notes feeling dirty in my hand, and left without another word. The bright sunlight of the piazza was a shock, feeling false and overly bright. The moment we were out of sight of the awning, around a corner and into the shelter of a narrow, shadowed *vicolo,* Enzo's composure cracked. He stopped walking, leaning against the nearest stone wall, and ran a hand over his face.

"*Dio mio,* Bianca. I should never have let you go down there alone. That was...that was too much."

"You didn't 'let' me," I shot back, quiet but firm, my own adrenaline seeking an outlet. "It was my choice. And...and it worked!" In the relative safety of the alley, I pulled out my phone, shielding the screen from any stray passersby. "Look."

When I opened the photos app, I handed my phone to him. He took it, his fingers brushing mine, and began to scroll. He stopped dead, his body going still. He scrolled through each photo slowly, his face tightening, the shock and dawning recognition breaking through his usual academic detachment. The false bottom, the heavy steel molds, the intricate forged seals, the press, each image was a nail in Carlo's coffin.

"Send them to me. Now," he said, his voice low and urgent, his eyes still fixed on the screen. "All of them. If anything happens, this doesn't vanish with us. It needs to exist in more than one place."

As I sent the files, a detail from my escape nagged at me. "Enzo, when I came out of the cellar...just as I was stepping out, I caught a movement from the corner of my eye. Down the hall, by the kitchen entrance."

He looked up from his phone, his focus sharpening. "Who was it?"

"It was Maria. She was just standing there, frozen. She saw me come out of the cellar, Enzo. She saw me lock it, and then she saw me open the bathroom door. She watched the whole thing and just nodded."

Enzo absorbed this, his expression turning grim. "And she didn't say a word? She didn't call for her uncle?"

"No. It was more than that," I said slowly, the memory crystallizing. "She didn't look angry or suspicious. She just looked...profoundly terrified. But not surprised to see *me*. It wasn't the look of someone catching a thief. It was the look of someone watching a prisoner attempt a jailbreak, terrified they'd be caught too. She was terrified *for* me."

Enzo was silent for a moment, weighing this. "His own niece," he murmured, shaking his head, the new layer of complexity dawning. "If she's a witness to your intrusion and remains silent...that changes everything we thought we knew about the inside of that house. It means there is a crack in Carlo's armor." He paused, thinking. "She had a clear choice. Raise the alarm and be the hero who caught the intruder, earning her uncle's favor. Or stay silent and become an accomplice. She chose silence. Hm. That's not the choice of a loyal niece."

"Exactly," I nodded, feeling a surge of conviction. "It was a choice made in a split second, and it tells us everything. She's not just scared *of* Carlo, I think...I felt as if she was trapped *by* him. She saw what I did, and she chose to let me get away with it. That's a connection, Enzo. A terrified, silent bond, but a bond nonetheless."

"Vespucci wasn't just unlucky," he continued, piecing it together further. "He was close. He must have really stumbled onto something."

"And someone made sure he'd never get a chance to share the truth," I finished, the memory of Carlo's cold hand on mine making me shiver despite the warm sun on my back.

"Now, I make and save copies," Enzo added, his tone leaving no room for argument, a plan solidifying in his mind. "Digital, physical. I'll get it to contacts in Rome...people who can't be swayed by Carlo's influence or his threats. We create a dead man's switch. If anything happens to either of us, the trail doesn't vanish. It explodes."

He fixed me with a stern, protective look. "And you —" he pointed a finger at me "— you open the gelateria tomorrow. First thing. You smile. You serve tourists. You scoop pistachio and lemon sorbet as if nothing in the world has happened. You are Bianca Moretti, the gelato girl, who knows nothing about cellars or forgeries, trying not to give him a single reason to look at you twice. You don't give him a reason to know how close you've come."

"Normal," I said, almost to myself, the word feeling foreign and impossible.

"It doesn't have to feel normal," he replied, his voice softening almost imperceptibly. "It just has to look it. It just has to keep you alive."

He pushed off from the wall, ready to go and begin his part of the work. He began to walk away, then paused, turning back to look at me.

"Bianca?"

"Yes?" I asked, my voice small in the narrow alley.

"Good work."

He disappeared around the corner, leaving me alone with the echo of his words. The unspoken *we* hung in the air, a delicate tie born out of the shadows we had shared.

On the walk home, I chose the longer path talong the beach, bending occasionally to pick up a shell, rugged and smoothed by the sea. The dazzling blue of the water and the raucous cries of the gulls felt this time like a taunt. The town's beauty was now harder to believe. The salt air tasted of secrets, and the sun on my back felt like a watchful eye. Clutching my keys, I reached my door. The closing of the lock sounded less like safety and more like a tomb sealing shut, the silence inside as heavy as the menace outside. The *we* was a distant shield, and I was alone with the chilling certainty that the town's walls had ears and its cellars held truths that could bury me.

Chapter 11

Echoes in the Alley

I forced a smile for the elderly couple, my hands moving on autopilot to scoop their cones of *stracciatella*. The morning sun streamed through the glass front of Dolce Vita, but I felt none of its warmth. Every sound, the hiss of the espresso machine, the chatter of tourists, seemed amplified, each one a potential prelude to a threat. I had to act normal. To show a flicker of the fear that was a constant hum in my veins would be a mistake I couldn't afford.

The transaction complete, I turned to wipe down the already-spotless counter, my mind replaying the sounds from the cellar, the look on Carlo's face in the trattoria. The proof on my phone felt less like a weapon and more like a bomb I was carrying in my apron pocket.

Just before noon, the bell chimed and Lucia entered, a splash of defiant color in a sage-green scarf. She planted herself on her usual stool. I placed a small porcelain cup of espresso before her. She accepted it, her sharp eyes fixed on the piazza outside.

Lucia stirred a single sugar cube into her espresso, the tiny spoon clinking rhythmically. After a few minutes, she spoke, her voice low and conspiratorial. “He’s been here four times since you opened.”

My chest tightened. I thought I knew, but still I asked, “Who?”

“Ettore.” She finally swiveled to look at me, her eyes alight with grim satisfaction. She picked up her *biscotto* and took a distracted bite, crumbs dusting the front of her cardigan. She didn't seem to notice. “He bought a newspaper, had a coffee, but the last two times, he just...stood.” She gestured with the remaining piece of biscuit towards the pharmacy. “He leans against the wall. Pretends to read flyers. Pretends to talk on his phone.” She leaned in closer, her voice dropping to a husky whisper. “His eyes don’t move, Bianca. He watches your door. He *waits*.”

She popped the last piece of *biscotto* into her mouth, brushing the crumbs from her fingers with a final, decisive slap against her thigh. “When you close up this evening, do not linger. Go straight home. Take the main street. And for once, *cara*, do not argue with me.”

The threat was now a man in a worn jacket, a tangible presence. The digital evidence on my phone felt flimsy against the physical reality of Ettore’s patrol.

The morning dragged on, each minute an agony of heightened awareness. I was a puppet going through the motions, my smile a stiff mask. My gelateria had become a trap.

Just after one o'clock, the bell chimed again. It was Enzo. He looked like he'd been up all night, shadows under his eyes, but his gaze was focused. He went to the gelato case, his back to the door.

"I need a kilo of the *fiore di latte*," he announced to the room. It was an absurd request, and his eyes signaled it was a code.

I nodded, pulling out a large tub and beginning to scoop. He leaned on the counter, his knuckles white.

"I sent the portfolio to my colleague in Rome last night," he informed me in a low voice, his eyes on the gelato. "The one at the university. I'm waiting for him to get back to me. It should be today." He let out a tense breath. "The waiting is...difficult."

I kept scooping, my head spinning. So we were still in limbo. Our evidence was still just a set of images in an inbox somewhere. "We need that confirmation, soon," I pressed quietly, stating the obvious.

"I know," he replied, his voice grim. "Without it, it's just our word. But he's a good man. He'll understand what he's looking at." He finally looked at me, and the full weight of his concern was in his eyes. "Just...watch yourself today."

Before I could formulate a response, a movement caught my eye. Reflected in the gleaming stainless steel of the espresso machine, I saw two women pause in the doorway, their eyes curious and quick, scanning the room before they decided to move on. To them, we would have looked like any other shopkeeper and customer, perhaps discussing a large order. But in the hyper-vigilant state we were in, the interruption broke our concentration, reminding us we were in the open, and that some of the countless eyes watching us could be Carlo's. They weren't entirely wrong to sense an intensity in the air, they were just misreading the context. We weren't simple conspirators. We stood there, aware of the fragility beneath the surface of our situation, both trying hard to pretend we didn't notice.

Enzo straightened up as I closed the tub. He paid in cash, his fingers lingered against mine as he took the heavy, chilled container. The touch was brief, but it conveyed everything his coded language could not: a caution, a care, an unspoken closeness between us. "Be careful," he said, his voice returning to a normal volume for the benefit of any unseen listeners. "Some things are more delicate than they appear. They can shatter if handled wrong."

And with that, he was gone, leaving me alone again with the chilling certainty that the walls were not just watching, but closing in.

The afternoon stretched on, an agonizing slow-motion parade of minutes, the heat gathering thick and heavy under the striped awning. I worked, the clack of spoons against metal pans a steady, mindless beat to keep my body moving forward while my mind raced in circles. At seven, as the sun began to dip behind the rooftops, the piazza finally thinned out, the tourists retreating to their hotels. I cleaned the last smears of chocolate from the gelato case, my movements slow and deliberate. I turned the sign to CHIUSO and locked the door with a definitive click that echoed through the silent shop. The sound felt to me like a cell door slamming shut.

I did as Enzo had urged. Keys gripped tight in my hand. Bag strapped securely across my body. But I was tired, soul-tired, and the longer, well-lit way home along the main thoroughfare felt like a marathon I didn't have the strength for. A dangerous apathy crept over me. *It's my town too,* I thought with a sudden, reckless defiance. I turned into the narrow, shadowed lane behind the pharmacy, the one I'd walked a thousand times during my childhood summers that I spent here in Cala d'Oro. I knew its every loose cobble, the way the plaster was peeling off the yellow wall near the bakery, the faint, clean smell of soap that always drifted from the vent of the laundress's ground-floor apartment.

Halfway down, the air changed. It wasn't the temperature. It was the *attention*. The feeling of being a mouse that has just sensed the still, focused presence of a cat. The hair on my arms stood up. The familiar lane suddenly felt alien and menacing.

I should have turned back. I should have run. But my feet, heavy with a strange, fatalistic inertia, kept walking. A shadow, deeper than the others, peeled itself away from the recessed doorway of a shuttered workshop. A rasp of metal on leather made me freeze, the sound unnaturally loud in the narrow space.

Ettore stepped forward, his usual limp strangely absent. In the dim, bluish light of the evening, a short, wicked knife glinted in his hand. It wasn't a kitchen knife, it was a tool for a darker purpose, with a worn handle and a blade that caught the light. He turned it slowly, almost lovingly, testing its edge with his thumb.

"You should be more careful, walking home all alone, *Signorina* Moretti," his voice deceptively almost gentle, a grotesque parody of concern. "The streets here are...uneven. Old. It's easy to have a bad accident." His smile was a thin, cruel line in his weathered face. "And the old one, Lucia...she talks too much for her own good. It would be a terrible shame if she slipped on those steep steps of hers. At her age, a fall can be...fatal."

"What do you want?" My voice was steadier than I felt, a small miracle.

"I'm just a messenger." The false gentleness evaporating, replaced by a flat, bitter menace. "Carlo says curiosity is a dangerous hobby in a town by the sea like ours. The tide takes what it wants, and no one ever finds it. No questions asked." His eyes, small and dark, locked on mine, trying to pin me in place. "You should leave town. Shut your shop. Sell it for whatever you can get. Go back to where you came from. People come and go here. Cala d'Oro forgets quickly, if you let it."

He leaned closer, and I caught the smell of stale smoke and cheap wine from his jacket. "You are not the first to stick your nose where it doesn't belong." He brought the knife up slightly, and I saw the tiny nicks and scars along the blade where it had been sharpened too many times, a history of violence etched into the steel. "The last one...he stopped breathing."

A reckless, borrowed courage, fueled by fear and fury, surged through me. "Was that before or after your boss cheated him with fake wine?" The words were out of my mouth before I could stop them, a direct hit from the arsenal of knowledge we'd gathered.

His face darkened, a storm cloud of rage passing over his features. The placid messenger vanished, replaced by open fury. He leaned in, his breath hot and foul on my ear. "Soon," he whispered, the word a venomous promise, "it will not matter, you will not matter."

Then, as quickly as he appeared, he retreated. He slid the knife back into his pocket, turned on his heel, and walked away. And I saw it clearly: his limp was almost gone, his stride quick, and purposeful. He did not limp when he wanted to be fast. He was gone, swallowed by the deepening shadows at the end of the lane, by the time a window squeaked open above us and an old woman I couldn't see shook a dust mop into the evening air.

I stood frozen for a long moment, too shaken to move. Gradually, the sharp edge of panic faded, and I could think clearly again. My first instinctive thought was of the police. *Call the carabinieri. Report him.* But the thought was immediately followed by a wave of cold, rational fear that was even more paralyzing.

Go to the local station? Tell my story to Sergeant Greco, who played cards with Carlo's cousin every Thursday? It would be my word against Ettore's. A story about a knife that left no mark, a threat with no witnesses. They would nod, make a note, and do nothing. Or worse, the first person Greco would call for a "friendly chat" would be Carlo himself. I'd be handing him confirmation that his intimidation had failed, and signing Lucia's death warrant in the process. The police weren't a shield, they were a sieve, and anything I poured into them would leak straight back to the man who wanted me gone.

The only safety for now, the only ally who understood the full, terrifying context, was Enzo.

I walked, not quickly, not slowly, but with a numb, mechanical determination, away from the main street and toward the museum, hoping Enzo would still be there. I didn't bother with the front door, with its heavy door and its public-facing openness. I used the side door that always creaked, a sound I would normally wince at, but now I didn't care who heard. Let them wonder. The pretense of normalcy was a thread that had just been severed by a knife's edge.

Enzo looked up from his desk, a magnifying glass in his hand, his reading glasses pushed into his disheveled hair. He took one look at my face, at the pallor I could feel beneath my skin, and was around the desk in an instant. "Bianca. What happened?"

The dam broke. "Ettore. In the lane behind the pharmacy. With a knife." The words tumbled out in a rushed, breathless stream. I told him everything, about the staged patrols Lucia had witnessed, the specific threat to her, the warning to leave town, the nicked blade, and the limp that turned into only the faintest trace of a hitch in his step.“ He said, ‘Soon it will not matter.’ I repeated the words, and they hung in the dusty, book-lined room like a death sentence.

Enzo was quiet for a long time, the only sound the gentle lapping of the sea outside. He stared into the middle distance, his historian’s mind undoubtedly connecting threads I couldn’t yet see. Finally, he let out a slow breath, the tension leaving his shoulders not with defeat, but with grim resolve.

“It’s not just a threat, Bianca,” his voice was low but carried in the hushed hall, a whisper among the silent ships in bottles. “It’s a reaction. Benedetti thought the whole unfortunate business would simply...fade away. A critic collapses in your gelateria? The town would talk, the shop would struggle, and eventually, it would become a sad little footnote. He never counted on you.” He gave me a small, appreciative smile. “He didn’t anticipate a former analyst from Milano with a talent for following trails and a fierce loyalty to her new home. You’ve poked a hornet’s nest by simply wanting to clear your own name.”

He walked to the window, looking out at the quiet canal. "That phone call about clearing the cellar...it makes even more sense now. He's not just tidying up. He is nervous and packing his entire operation, for now at least. You've made this town too hot for his secrets, and he's scrambling to erase them before your curiosity uncovers what he's truly been hiding in the shadows of this lovely little town."

Enzo stopped pacing and looked at me, his expression softening from alarm to a quiet, steadfast determination. "It's time, Bianca." His voice remained calm but firm, a steady anchor in the swirling uncertainty. "We lay it all out for Marco. Your photos, the ledger pages, everything, the whole story. We may not have the final confirmation from Rome yet, but we have enough to paint a picture. A picture of a threat against you, and a secret in a cellar that has nothing to do with gelato."

He was right, of course. It was the logical next step. But the thought of handing over our precious, hard-won clues, entrusting the fate of my shop and my new life to the cautious, inscrutable *carabiniere* who had as if taken the place of my childhood friend, Marco, sent a fresh chill through me, colder than the air surrounding the museum's preserved treasures.

Enzo walked me home, and for once i did not object. A silent, protective presence at my side, his eyes constantly scanning the shadows. At my door, he didn't leave until he heard the deadbolt slide into place with a solid, metallic thud.

Inside, the familiar walls of my apartment offered no comfort. I didn't bother with tea or food. I went straight to the small wooden box I kept on my bookshelf and spread its contents across my kitchen table like a tarot reading of my own peril: the printed photos, the copies of the ledger pages, the rain-smudged note from the gutter. I laid my phone beside them, the screen glowing, showing the damning, flash-illuminated images of Carlo's forgeries.

The wind lifted the curtain, carrying the relentless, whispering sound of the sea. Out in the alley, a cat screeched, a sound of sudden violence that made me jump.

Soon it will not matter, Ettore's voice echoed in the silent room.

I looked at the pieces of the story laid out before me, each one a risk taken, each one a truth fought for. The fear was still there, a shard of ice in my chest. But as I looked at the evidence, at the story of Lazzaro and Carlo, of Vespucci and the forged wine, something else was rising to meet the fear, something hard and determined and fiercely protective of this town I called home now.

Soon, I thought, my fingers tracing the image of a steel mold for a Château Lafite seal, *I will make it matter.*

Chapter 12

Calculated Risk

Enzo's declaration in the museum hung in the silent air. *It's time.* The decision was made. We were hurtling toward a confrontation, and the path ahead led directly to Marco. The man whose last name was Rossi, like Ettore's.

Sleep was impossible. The night became a long rehearsal of what we would say, how we would present our case. I imagined Marco's face, the professional mask, the weary eyes, the possible flicker of familial loyalty that could undermine everything.

Dawn broke not with comfort, but with the grim light of that impending meeting. The luxury of waiting for Rome's confirmation, for a safer moment, had evaporated with the glint of the knife.

My phone buzzed on the nightstand, an expected signal. Enzo's name glowed on the screen. *Da Gino. Lunch.*

No further details were needed. Enzo had managed it. He had secured the meeting. Something like a stage fright clenched my chest, the audience was waiting for a role I didn't know I could play.

Da Gino was a world away from the polished, oppressive elegance of Benedetti's. Tucked down a narrow alley that perpetually smelled of burnt garlic and brine, it was a place of honest simplicity. It wasn't fancy here, and that was the charm. The chairs were mismatched — some painted a peeling green, others polished smooth by decades of use — and the walls carried a jumble of history: a cracked print of the Madonna, a shelf of dust-softened wine bottles, a string of garlic bulbs hanging tiredly above the bar. Someone had tucked sprigs of rosemary into empty carafes on the counter, so the air smelled faintly of resin even after the mop had wiped away the day's rush. It was the kind of place that seemed to shrug at gossip and storms alike, as if it knew it would still be here long after we'd come and gone.

We were sitting at the corner table, the one with a checked cloth more faded than the rest, its edges fraying like an old postcard. The manila folder sat between us like a loaded weapon. Inside lay our hard-won collected pieces, we thought would sway Marco to action.

We'd finished bowls of *pasta e fagioli* and were letting the last of the house red linger in our glasses. The broth had been thick with beans and rosemary, the kind of food that left warmth behind even after the plates were cleared.

"It's better than anything in Bologna," Enzo had declared, though with a mock-seriousness that made me roll my eyes.

"Better than Bologna? Careful there," I said. "You'll have to issue a statement at the next Cala d'Oro cultural council meeting."

He smirked, swirling his glass. "Then I'll stand by it."

The folder on the table seemed to radiate a nervous energy of its own. I couldn't stop my eyes from flicking towards it as we ate, then to the door, then to Enzo's face. He was attempting to appear calm, as if we were here just for a casual lunch, but a faint tremor in his hand as he reached for his wine glass betrayed him. The adrenaline from the previous night had burned away, leaving behind a brittle, exhausted resolve. The lively clatter of pans from the kitchen felt like a mockery of the silent dread pressing in on us.

"He will come," Enzo murmured finally, his voice low enough that only I could hear it over the murmur of the other patrons, a pair of old men arguing about football by the window. "He agreed. He understands the seriousness."

A knot of doubt tightened in my stomach. "Does he?" I whispered back, my fingers tracing a sticky ring on the checked cloth. "Or does he just understand that we're a problem he needs to manage? We're about to hand him everything, Enzo. Everything we've risked our necks for. What if his first loyalty isn't to the law, but to the Rossi name?" The unspoken names hung in the air between us: *Ettore Rossi. Matteo Rossi.*

Enzo finally looked up from his plate, his gaze steadying me. "Then we will know. And we will act accordingly. But we must give him the chance. He is the only authority we can approach."

But was he? The authority he represented felt distant, slow-moving, bound in red tape. The threat Ettore represented was immediate, visceral, and lurking just outside the door. I felt a sudden, wild impulse to grab the folder and run, to handle this ourselves. It was a mad thought, one that grew from the stubborn, gnawing feeling that this meeting was a mistake. Were we walking into a trap and then, unbelievably, showing our cards — the detailed plans for escape?

The trattoria's door clicked shut softly, as Marco entered. He wasn't in uniform, but wore dark trousers and a crisp, navy polo shirt that carried an air of officialdom. He didn't need to scan the room. His eyes, shadowed with a fatigue that mirrored our own sleepless nights, found us instantly. He moved with a weary purpose, nodding once to the old men at the window, who fell silent and watched him pass with a mixture of respect and curiosity. He was a local boy made good, a fixture in the community. And we were the outsiders about to accuse his blood.

He slid into the wooden chair opposite us, the groan of the wood under his weight the only fanfare for this clandestine meeting. He placed his phone face-down on the table, a silent signal that his attention was, for now, ours. His gaze swept over me, and I saw a flicker of something — concern? Annoyance? — before his expression settled into a neutral, professional mask.

"Bianca. Enzo," he began, his voice a low, gravelly baritone. "You said it was urgent."

Enzo gave a slight, tense nod. "It is." He nudged the folder an inch closer to Marco. "There was an incident last night."

I found my voice, though it felt thin and reedy. "Ettore Rossi cornered me in the alley behind the pharmacy. He had a knife." The words tumbled out, and I forced myself to slow down, to meet Marco's gaze directly. I needed him to see the truth of it, to see the fear that was still a live wire under my skin. "He told me to leave town. He said it would be a 'terrible shame' if Lucia had a 'fatal' fall on her steps." Just repeating the threat made my palms damp. "This isn't just about old ledgers anymore, Marco. He threatened an old woman's life to get to me."

Marco's face remained impassive, but a muscle in his jaw twitched. He didn't reach for the folder. Instead, he steepled his fingers on the table, his focus entirely on me. "Start from the beginning. Leave nothing out."

And so we did. We laid out the entire, tangled story. I spoke of my growing suspicions about the cannery fire and Marco's uncle, Matteo. Enzo detailed our visit to the boathouse, the Lazzarus, and our aborted attempt to follow Ettore. I described the tension in the air at Benedetti's, the overheard phone call about moving "material" from the cellar. Then, my voice dropping even lower, I confessed to slipping into the cellar itself, the discovery of the forgery tools, the feverish photography. Enzo interjected to explain the significance of the dies and plates, the tell-tale marks of a professional counterfeiting operation.

Throughout it all, Marco listened. He didn't interrupt, didn't scoff, didn't react beyond that occasional tic in his jaw. His silence was more unnerving than any outburst. He was a sponge, absorbing every detail, his dark, unreadable eyes fixed on us. I felt like a suspect under a harsh interrogation lamp, my every word being weighed and measured for inconsistencies.

When we finally fell silent, the only sound was the distant sizzle of food from the kitchen. The folder, still unopened, sat as a testament to our risk. Marco leaned back in his chair, the wood creaking in protest.

"You're asking me," he started, his tone dangerously calm, "to launch an official investigation based on a series of illegal actions. Breaking and entering. Theft of private documents." He ticked the points off on his fingers. "You have no witness to this alleged knife attack. You have photographs taken during an unlawful search. You have ledger pages that, by your own admission, you stole."

"We *copied* them," Enzo corrected, a flush of frustration rising on his neck. "And we did what we had to do because a man died, Marco! Claudio Vespucci collapsed in Bianca's shop." He leaned forward, his voice intensifying. "But this isn't just about how he died. It's about where he died. You told her yourself when she reopened, gelato might be clear, but it doesn't wash a stain from a reputation. You know that the town will always remember it all started in *her* gelateria, until they have a real answer, a real culprit! Every question we asked, every small thread we pulled, it all led back to one place. We didn't target Benedetti, the trail itself led us to his door...we are just trying to give the town that answer."

"What you *knew*," Marco countered, his voice hardening, "were suspicions. What you *did* was break the law. My job is to uphold the law, not to act on...on a hunch!" He gestured dismissively at the folder. "This is a collection of interesting scraps. Without something official, like a verifiable authentication from Rome, it's nothing I can act on. It's conjecture. It's a story."

The dismissal was like a physical blow. All the risk, the terror of the night before, reduced to "a story." I could feel the heat of humiliation and anger rising in my cheeks. "A story?" I repeated, my voice trembling. "Ettore's knife wasn't a story. The fear in that alley was very real. Carlo Benedetti is moving that evidence by end of the week, we heard it! If we wait for your 'procedure,' it will be gone. Forever. And what happens to Lucia then? Is her safety just another 'scrap'?"

Marco's eyes flashed, and for a second, the professional mask slipped, revealing a glimpse of the exasperated man beneath. "Do not put words in my mouth, Bianca. I am telling you the reality of the situation. I cannot mobilize resources based on this. I need more. I need experts. I do not have the authority to act on shadows and hearsay."

The silence that followed was thick and suffocating. The old men at the window had returned to their argument, their voices a jarringly normal sound in our bubble of tension. I felt a surge of despair. He wasn't going to help us. We had laid our souls bare, and he was dismissing it all as irrelevant, as a nuisance.

Then, Marco leaned forward again, his elbows on the table, his voice dropping to a whisper so faint I had to lean in to hear. He was breaching protocol, and he knew it. "What matters now, more than your forgeries, is this: Claudio Vespucci didn't die by chance or any natural causes."

The shift was so jarring it left me momentarily speechless. We were talking about an imminent crime, a desperate plea, and a knife in an alley, and he was dragging us back to the poison.

Enzo, ever the academic, caught up quickly on the new data. "Ah...so, the toxicology report finally came back?"

Marco hesitated. His eyes flicked toward the door, then back to us. He lowered his voice even further. "It's confirmed. Vespucci was poisoned. Deliberately."

The word landed not with a bang, but with a sickening, silent thud in the quiet room. *Poisoned.* It was the confirmation I had desperately wanted, the thing that should have cleared my name from the shadow of incompetence. But in this context, delivered as a rebuttal to our pleas, it felt like a trap. It was a piece of information he could control, a single, manageable thread he could pull to keep the narrative focused on a crime that had already happened as some saw it — murder — in my gelateria, and away from the vast, dangerous conspiracy that was unfolding in the present.

"What kind?" I managed to ask, the memory of the critic's fall and his gasping moments fighting for life in my shop flooding back with horrifying clarity.

He rubbed a hand across his stubbled jaw, his gaze avoiding mine. "Something potent." He exhaled, a long, weary sigh. "I shouldn't be telling you this. It's...not procedure. But you need to understand the stakes. I have a confirmed homicide."

There it was. The careful, calculated bone. Giving us just enough to make us feel included, to keep us compliant, but not enough to truly let us into the inner circle. The folder with its proof of a larger, ongoing crime sat between us, unopened and ignored. He had the bigger, more immediate piece now, the confirmed murder, and he was using it to steer the conversation back to a path where he held all the cards, a path that required patience and procedure, two things we no longer possessed.

Enzo leaned forward, his tone measured but insistent, refusing to be fully diverted. "So the question remains, Marco...who decided a food critic's palate was too discerning? Who decided Claudio Vespucci needed permanent silencing?" His gaze held Marco's, and for the first time, the question felt less like a query and more like a direct challenge. It was a question that led directly to the man whose enforcer wielded a knife in the dark.

Marco's fingers tapped once, decisively, on the table. The moment of vulnerability was gone, replaced by the stern officer again. "That is the question my investigation will answer. But it will answer it with evidence that will stand up in a court of law. Not with photos from a cellar I have no warrant to search." It was a bureaucratic answer, a deflection. He was treating a kingpin like a common suspect in a single, isolated crime.

He pushed back his chair, the legs scraping loudly against the terracotta tiles. He stood, leaving the folder untouched, a silent, profound rejection of our evidence, our risk, our desperation.

"That's all for now," he announced, his voice returning to its official, impersonal tone. "The information about the poisoning does not leave this table. Stay out of the investigation. Do not confront Carlo. Do not go near that boathouse. I'm not asking."

He didn't wait for a reply, didn't look back. He turned and walked out. In the sudden silence that followed, the two of us were left with the unopened, damning evidence, sitting in a cloud of unresolved tension.

The warmth of the trattoria had vanished. The honest smells of tomatoes and rosemary now seemed cloying, suffocating. I stared at the empty chair, at the space where Marco had been. The *carabiniere* captain was gone, and in his place was the ghost of Marco Rossi, my childhood friend whose family ties seemed to bind him tighter than any oath of office.

Enzo finally reached for his wine glass, his hand trembling slightly. He took a long drink, then set it down with a quiet click. "He gave us the toxicology to placate us," he murmured, his eyes fixed on the empty doorway. "A bone to gnaw on so we'd stop barking up the bigger tree. His caution makes procedural sense, but it's a luxury we don't have."

I pressed my palms flat against the frayed, sticky tablecloth. Marco's dismissal was a stark reminder of a truth I'd been trying to ignore. "He's not going to help us," I whispered, the words tasting of ash. "Not yet. A cleared gelato doesn't un-ruin my life in the eyes of this town. It doesn't stop Ettore." I glanced toward the door, the ghost of Marco's departure still lingering. "His 'procedure' is a shield. But is it protecting the law, or the Rossi name?"

Enzo let out a long, weary breath, his gaze fixed on the untouched folder. "His hands are tied without Rome's confirmation. He said it himself. It means nothing to him until then." He finally looked at me, his expression not one of defiant certainty, but of grim calculation. "But if that confirmation comes...if experts put their names to those photos, it just could change the game. It might be enough to force his hand, to make his procedure work for us instead of against us."

A fragile thread of hope, thin as a spider's silk, wove itself through my resolve. "So we wait for Rome?" The idea felt like agony.

"Hm. We prepare," Enzo countered, his voice low and steady. "We watch. We know the timeline — by end of the week, the boathouse. If Rome replies in time, we try Marco again. We can give him one last chance to do the right thing." He leaned forward, his eyes holding mine with an unspoken question. "But if Friday comes and Rome is silent...then we have a decision to make. A very dangerous one."

The fight was far from over, but its shape had changed. It was no longer a simple plea, it was a strategic delay, a tense waiting game with a deadly deadline. The unopened file was no longer just a battle plan. It was a test. A test of Rome's efficiency, and ultimately, a test of Marco's character. And what calmed me was that I knew we would be ready for the outcome, whatever it turned out to be.

Chapter 13

Playing the Part

The silence between Enzo and me as we left Trattoria da Gino had weight and texture, it felt like walking through seawater, each step requiring effort against its resistance. Marco's dismissal hadn't been a simple 'no.' It felt like a door being firmly shut, locking us out of the investigation with a quiet, final click. The folder in my bag, once so full of promise, now felt like a brick.

We walked back to the Dolce Vita in a tense, wordless procession. The post-storm clarity of the town seemed to mock our confusion, the way the sunlight caught the raindrops on geranium petals, the too-bright shimmer of wet cobblestones. My fingers, numb with a chill that had nothing to do with the weather, fumbled with the keys to the gelateria. The door swung inward, and we stepped out of the bright, exposed *piazza* and into the gelateria's stillness.

Inside, the silence felt different from the morning's peaceful quiet. This was a charged silence, thick with suspense. The only sign of my previous life was the faint, clean smell of the floor I had mopped just hours ago. That simple chore felt like it belonged to another person, from a time when my biggest worry was the sugar ratio in the lemon sorbet.

Seeking comfort my hands moved stacking receipt rolls into a perfect cylinder, twisting espresso cups until their handles all pointed to the same precise angle. Each motion was a silent prayer for an order that had vanished from my world. I shoved the rejected folder deep under the counter, behind a box of spare lids. *Out of sight, out of mind*, I told myself. It was a lie, of course, I knew.

Enzo leaned against the service counter, his jacket slung over a chair. His arms were crossed, and the patient look of the historian was gone, replaced by sharp frustration that seemed to make the air crackle.

"You're very quiet," he observed, his voice a low rumble that cut through the hum of the freezers.

"He didn't just say no, Enzo," I burst out, slamming the cutlery drawer shut. The clatter was shockingly loud. "He made us complicit! Dangling the fact that it was poison — 'something strong' — in front of us, and then telling us to go home. Now I'm looking at every ingredient here as a potential weapon. Almond extract? Cyanide. Bitter apricot kernels? The same. It's cruel."

Enzo's mouth formed a grimace that held no warmth. "Yes. He gives just enough information to keep us terrified," he added, his voice soft but unyielding. "Think, Bianca. He arrives at the scene with astonishing speed. He shares with us a toxicology report in a trattoria, not even in his office. And then...then he even refuses to open our folder of clues about Carlo's operations. Is that procedure, or...is it rather a man cutting a thread he doesn't want pulled?"

The doubt, spelled out in words like this, began to twist through my certainty. I yanked open the coin drawer, pointlessly lining up euros and cents into neat stacks. "He was on the square for a meeting when Vespucci collapsed. It was a coincidence."

"This town runs on coincidences the way my old boat runs on wishes and good intentions, eh?" a dry voice cut in from the doorway.

A cheerful chime announced *Zia* Lucia's arrival as she stepped into the room. Her cardigan was buttoned crookedly and her silver bun was slightly askew, as if she'd rushed over. She took in the scene with one sharp glance, Enzo's intensity, my frantic tidying, the charged silence.

"You look like a woman who's been listening to bad news," she announced, lowering herself onto her customary stool with a soft groan. She patted the space beside her. "Come. Sit. Standing there won't change the weather."

"I'm a woman who's been listening to Enzo pick apart every word Marco said until I don't know what to believe anymore," I said, the weariness filling my voice.

Lucia sniffed. "Hmph. Same thing." She turned to Enzo. "Well? Out with it. The air in here is sour enough to curdle milk. What did the good captain have to say?"

"He confirmed it was poison," Enzo said flatly. "Then he refused to look at our evidence and told us to go home."

Lucia's eyes widened a fraction. "He told you? Outright?" She folded her arms, a gesture of deep suspicion. "When your Nonna was alive, the police kept their lips sealed tighter than a miser's purse. For a captain to talk so freely...hm, it isn't proof of guilt, *cara*, but it isn't normal either."

Enzo nodded grimly. "It feels almost like a performance, designed to neutralize us."

Lucia's gaze drifted past me, out to the *piazza* and the gleaming sea in the distance. "A fast response can be care. A good man doing his job well." She paused, her eyes turning inward, accessing some old memory. "But fast can also mean he knew what he would find before he arrived. I remember when old

Signor Ricci died, the fisherman, not the nephew, the *carabinieri* were there before his wife had even finished screaming. Turns out they'd been watching his boat for weeks, waiting." She reached out and pressed her warm hand over mine, stilling its nervous motion. "Don't close your eyes to a puzzle just because you like the picture on the box."

The door swung open again. Paolo from the docks shuffled in, his eyes searching. "*Signora*," he said, nodding at Lucia. He worried the rim of his cap. "I've been looking for you. There is talk."

"You are always looking for me, Paolo, and there is always talk," Lucia muttered, their ancient dance.

He leaned closer. "The officer is asking again. The one with the square shoulders. Down by the bait shop, talking to old Nando. Wants to know who saw what, before the critic died. Wants to know about crates."

Enzo and I exchanged a swift glance. *Square shoulders*. Marco.

"Which officer, Paolo?" I asked, struggling to sound casual.

"The one who drinks the long coffee and never finishes it. The captain." His eyes darted between us. "I can walk you back, if you like. Seems like there's talk everywhere."

She gave a small, dismissive snort. “Bah! You don’t want to walk me anywhere, Paolo. You want an excuse to linger and listen. Go buy your anchovies and stop hopping about like a sparrow.”

When he was gone, the silence felt louder. Enzo straightened up, his whole body alert. “If Marco is down by the water *after* sending us away...He’s either investigating Carlo, or he’s making a very public show of it.” He grabbed his jacket. “I need to know which it is. Stay here. Both of you.”

"Go, go," Lucia said slowly, her voice quiet. "The silence in this room is getting loud, and I don't like what it's starting to say!"

He gave a terse nod and was gone.

The next thirty minutes stretched slow and sticky with anxiety. Lucia had moved behind the counter with me, her presence both comforting and unnerving. She began methodically checking expiration dates on syrups, her movements economical and sure.

"You're worrying the stone off that counter, eh," she observed without looking at me.

I hadn't realized I'd been running my hand back and forth along the marble counter's edge. "I can't stand this waiting."

"Waiting is part of life, Bianca. Like breathing." She set down a bottle of hazelnut syrup. "When your

Nonna was alive, we spent more time waiting than doing. Waiting at the market, waiting for weather, waiting for news from the mainland." She finally looked at me, her eyes soft with memory. "The waiting changes you, *ragazza*, it either makes you frantic," she gestured to my restless hands, "or it makes you ready."

"What did it make you?" I asked, genuinely curious.

She considered this, wiping a cloth over a nonexistent spot on the counter. "Me? Hm. It made me practical. I learned to use the waiting time. To prepare." Her eyes met mine, and in them I saw the young woman she'd been, tough, resilient, weathered by more than sea salt and sun. "Whatever Enzo finds, you will need to be ready. Not just afraid."

The hum of the freezers seemed to agree. I took a deep breath, trying to absorb some of her practicality, her stillness that calmed me.

Finally, Enzo was back, smelling of sea and diesel. His face was neutral, but frustration simmered beneath the surface.

“Well?” Lucia demanded. “Does our captain seek the truth, or is he merely gardening?”

Enzo let out a short breath. “Nando talks too much and says nothing. He ‘might have’ seen a crate, ‘or perhaps a small box?’ late that night.

No description. No specific time. It's the kind of testimony that keeps an inquiry active on paper, but goes nowhere." He looked at me. "He could be building a case, or he could be building a wall."

The frustration was a weight on my chest. We were circling the truth, but it remained just out of reach.

The rest of the day was an exercise in tension. Customers provided a fleeting distraction. Every time the door opened, my head snapped up. Was it Marco? A thug from Carlo? Serving gelato had become a nerve-wracking ordeal.

During the afternoon lull, I was in the back refilling the pistachio paste when the door opened. The sound was soft, but as if the atmosphere in the shop shifted instantly, growing dense and cold.

It wasn't a customer.

Carlo Benedetti stood just inside the doorway. He wasn't looking at the menu. His gaze was fixed on me, a slow, comprehensive inventory that left me feeling defenseless.

"*Buongiorno*, Bianca," he said. His voice was like polished stone, smooth and devoid of warmth.

My throat tightened. "*Signor* Benedetti," I managed.

He took a few slow steps, his eyes sweeping over the shop as if inspecting his domain. "I hear the reopening is going well. *Brava.* The town needs its little comforts, especially with all this...troubles." He paused. "I also heard you had an...an unsettling evening. My apologies. Some of my associates are simple men. They can be overzealous."

The audacity was staggering. He was apologizing for a terror he had orchestrated.

In that moment, Lucia's words about being ready, not just afraid, echoed in my mind. In a split-second decision, I decided to play the part of the flattered, frightened shopkeeper, gelato Bianca, hoping Benedetti believes it. I let my shoulders slump slightly and allowed a tremor to enter my voice. "It was a misunderstanding, I'm sure," I said, letting a tremor enter my voice. "What can I do for you?"

"I am glad you are so reasonable," he said, his lips curving into a cool smile. "Which is why I am here. To make amends. You can join me for dinner tonight. At my trattoria. A private table. To ensure we have a clear understanding about your future here."

It was a summons, not an invitation, that much I understood. Refusing was not an option.

I forced a flustered smile. "Thank you. That is...very kind. It would be terribly discourteous to refuse."

Satisfaction flashed in his eyes. “Excellent. Eight o’clock.” Then, with eerie normality, he pointed to the gelato case. “I will have a scoop of the lemon. To go.”

He paid, told me to keep the change, and left. The door closed with a soft, final click.

The moment he was gone, my legs felt weak. I leaned heavily against the counter, trembling. I pulled out my phone, my fingers shaking.

Me: Carlo was just here. Dinner. Tonight. At his trattoria.

The three dots pulsed for an eternity.

Enzo: Bianca no! You cannot! It’s a trap!

Me: If I refuse, he wins! He knows I’m intimidated, this is the only move Marco has left us. I have to go.

Enzo: This is madness! We should try Marco again!

Me: And say what? That I’m scared because the town’s most powerful man invited me to dinner? It proves nothing. No. I go. I play my part. And you’ll be watching.

The door burst open. Enzo strode in, his face pale. He came behind the counter, his hand on my arm, his voice urgent. “Bianca, no. This is different. We have to tell Marco.”

"I know what it is," I said, my voice steadier than I felt. "But don't you see? He expects me to be terrified. So I won't be. Or at least, I won't show it. I'll be flattered. Naive. I'll play the part of a woman who's in over her head but too foolish to know it." I met his worried gaze squarely. "It's the only move we have left."

He saw the determination in my eyes, a determination born from the sheer frustration with our situation. He knew he couldn't dissuade me. His shoulders slumped in defeat, but he gripped my arm tightly, a anchor in the sudden storm. "Then we do this my way. I'll be on the church steps across the square from eight-thirty. I will be watching the door. If you are not out by ten, I am coming in. I don't care about Carlo, I don't care about Marco, and I don't care about the consequences. Do you understand me?"

I nodded, a lump forming in my throat. His protectiveness was a warm cloak in the chilling situation. "I understand."

He pulled me into a brief, fierce hug. "*Stai attenta*, Bianca," he whispered into my hair. Stay safe.

Then he released me and was gone, leaving me alone in the silent gelateria. The cheerful, colorful space now felt like a staging ground for a battle I never wanted to fight. The clock on the wall ticked relentlessly, each second a step closer to eight o'clock, and my dinner date with the most dangerous man in Cala d'Oro.

Chapter 14

Quiet Divide

There was no point in staying open. I closed up early, but the familiar routine of locking the door brought no sense of closure for the day, only the heavy awareness of being closer to the appointment I still had to keep. The lively chatter from the street seemed to mock the unease settling in my stomach.

Back in my apartment above the tailor's shop, the silence was a heavy blanket. I stood before my wardrobe, a divided archive of my life. On one side hung the practical, sun-bleached cottons and comfortable linens of my new existence in Cala d'Oro, the uniform of a gelateria owner. On the other, a few carefully preserved relics from my old life in Milan: sleek silhouettes of black, navy, and charcoal grey.

The longer I stared into my closet, the more my plan to play the simple *gelataia* started crumbling. That role felt flimsy, a paper shield against a man like Carlo. He'd see it for the performance it was, and my perceived naivete would only make me look foolish. No. To survive this, I needed a different kind of armor. My fingers brushed past simple sundresses and settled on a relic from my old life: a ruthlessly minimalist black sheath dress. Slipping it on, the heavy crepe felt both alien and familiar — a skin I'd shed, but not forgotten. It was a piece from another era, purchased for client dinners and gallery openings, where perception was a currency as important as euro. It felt alien against the sun-warmed skin of my arms, a reminder of the polished, guarded woman I'd been. In Milan, this dress was a statement of competence and cool detachment. Tonight, in Cala d'Oro, it sent a silent message to Carlo: *I understand power. I am a woman you should not underestimate.*

I applied a bare minimum of makeup, just enough to keep from looking washed out, and fastened my late Nonna's simple gold cross around my neck, a tiny, defiant talisman of the good I still believed existed in this town. At ten minutes to eight, a nervous glance in the mirror confirmed the image: composed, serious, and utterly terrified beneath the surface.

The walk to Trattoria Benedetti passed in a blur. The evening air was soft, carrying the scent of jasmine and the distant murmur of the sea. It was a perfect spring night, a backdrop for romance and leisurely strolls, not for a clandestine dinner with a potential killer. I pushed open the heavy, dark-wood door of the trattoria and stepped inside.

It was a stage set of rustic opulence and warmth, a stark contrast to the ice in my veins. Copper pots gleamed from racks overhead. The walls were lined with racks of wine, their dark glass bottles glowing like jewels in the soft light. The air was thick with the rich, comforting aromas of garlic, roasting meat, and simmering tomatoes. Laughter and the clink of glasses rose from the packed tables. It was the picture of Italian conviviality.

My entrance caused a palpable ripple. Conversations stuttered, eyes flicked toward me, curious and wary. I felt like a black swan that had landed in a pond of brightly colored ducks. Carlo rose from a secluded corner table, partially screened by a large, gnarled olive tree in a terracotta pot. He was a picture of avuncular charm, his smile wide and welcoming, an expression utterly belied by the predatory, assessing calculation in his eyes.

"Ah, Bianca," he said, his voice a low purr. He didn't move to pull out my chair immediately. Instead, his gaze traveled over me, from my heels to the severe line of my dress, a slow, appreciative inventory that felt more invasive than complimentary.

"I must admit, I was expecting the girl from the gelateria. But this..." He made a small, elegant gesture. "This is a surprise. A very...very compelling surprise."

He finally pulled out my chair, his hand lingering on the back of it as I sat. "The dress is Milan, no? Armani, perhaps? It suits you far better than aprons."

"Thank you for having me, *Signor* Benedetti," I said, my voice carefully neutral, ignoring the probe.

He poured the wine himself, a deep, blood-red Nero d'Avola. "From the slopes of Etna. The soil there is volcanic, ash and rock. It forges something complex and resilient from hardship." His eyes met mine over the rim of his glass. "Much like people, don't you think? It seems we both have hidden depths, *Signorina* Bianca."

The dinner was a spectacle of carefully staged opulence, where the taste of truffles and the weight of silverware were intertwined with an occasional veiled threat. The antipasti arrived, a breathtaking spread that was a work of art. Paper-thin slices of *culatello*, the prized ham, were draped over the plate like delicate rose petals. Fat, green Cerignola olives swam in a pool of golden olive oil studded with rosemary and chili. There were roasted artichoke hearts with slivers of lemon zest, and tiny, sweet onions caramelized in balsamic vinegar. Carlo spoke of the provenance of each ingredient as if narrating a sacred text.

The *primo* was a sublime *pasta alle vongole*. The spaghetti was perfectly al dente, tossed with dozens of tiny, sweet clams that had been steamed open in a sauce of white wine, garlic, and a hint of chili. It tasted purely of the sea, a simple, perfect dish that, under any other circumstances, would have been a revelation. Carlo held forth on the quality of the anchovies this season, the folly of the mayor's new zoning laws, the simple, efficient pleasures of a well-run town. I played my part, the appreciative guest, offering small, harmless replies. "The clams are delicious." "Yes, the mayor's plan does seem impractical." My mind, however, was racing, searching every pleasantry for a hidden barb.

Throughout the meal, I was acutely aware of Carlo's niece, Maria. She was a silent, flitting presence, a ghost in her own family's restaurant. Her face was pale, her eyes wide and perpetually startled, like a rabbit caught in a snare. She moved between the tables with a quiet efficiency, but her hands trembled slightly when she cleared plates. When she brought the main course — a magnificent *branzino*, its skin crisped to a golden brown, nestled on a bed of shaved fennel and blood orange slices — the atmosphere at our table shifted. Carlo was called away to the bar to greet an important-looking couple, leaving me alone for a precious moment.

This was her chance. Maria approached the table, her movements stiff with a tension that was painful to watch. The plate rattled faintly in her hand as she set it down before me. Her eyes met mine for a fraction of a second, and in them, I saw pure, undiluted fear. It was a look that stripped away all my own feelings and replaced it with a fierce, protective urge. As she leaned over to adjust the placement of the plate, her body strategically blocking the view from the rest of the room, her starched white apron pocket brushed my arm. It was a clumsy, natural movement. But as she pulled away, I felt it: the crisp corner of a folded piece of paper pressed into my hand.

A jolt of adrenaline shot through me. I didn't flinch, didn't gasp. I simply gave a small, polite nod. "Grazie, Maria."

She fled back toward the kitchen without a word. I waited a beat, then casually dropped my napkin. Bending down, my fingers properly grabbed the note in the palm of my hand, the paper feeling like a live coal. I tucked it safely into the small clutch purse on my lap.

Carlo returned, his eyes narrowing slightly. "You seem...hm, distracted? I hope the conversation hasn't bored you."

"Not at all," I said. "I was just admiring the art on the walls." The lie came smoothly, the Milanese professional effortlessly taking over.

I pleaded fatigue as soon as it was socially acceptable. Carlo, with an air of magnanimous victory, saw me to the door. "I trust we have an understanding, Bianca," he said, his voice oily with false concern. He placed a heavy hand on my shoulder. "It has been a true pleasure discovering the woman behind the counter. Let's ensure she has a bright future here. Sleep well."

The words were a threat wrapped in a blessing. I merely nodded, not trusting myself to speak, and stepped out into the blessedly fresh night air.

Enzo was on the church steps as he promised, a silhouette of anxiety, equipped with a stiff manila envelope. He strode toward me, his eyes searching my face in the dim light.

"Are you alright? What did he do?"

"I'm fine. He just...talked." His hand came up, his thumb gently brushing a stray wisp of hair from my cheek, a gesture so intimate it stole my breath. "You were in there too long. I was going out of my mind." The concern in his voice, the warmth of his touch after Carlo's cool appraisal, was my undoing. A tremor I'd been holding back all evening ran through me. He saw it, and his expression softened with a tenderness that made my heart ache.

"I'm alright," I repeated, my voice barely a whisper. He didn't remove his hand, instead letting it slide to my shoulder, a steadying anchor. "Come on. Let's get out of the light." We walked in silence, the sounds of the trattoria fading behind us. Only when we were two streets away, sheltered in the deep, concealing darkness of a narrow *vicolo* where the buildings leaned close enough to whisper, did I stop.

"Well?" His voice was tight with anticipation. "How was the lion's den?"

"The lion was on his best behavior," I whispered, feeling a relief, although my hands still shaking. I fumbled in my purse, my fingers finally closing around the folded square of paper. "But one of the lion's cubs seems to have something on her mind." I handed it to him. "Maria."

Under the sliver of moonlight that managed to filter down into the alley, we unfolded the note and read the rushed, desperate script.

He is moving everything. The crates from the cellar and the boathouse. Friday evening, after dark. To the old boathouse dock. A boat named 'Stella Maris' will be there. He is nervous. The men are angry. I am so scared! I know too much! – M

"No! His own niece!" I exclaimed, the pieces snapping into a grotesque picture. "She's risking everything!"

Enzo looked up from the note, his eyes blazing with a mixture of fury and triumph. "It's more than a risk, Bianca, it's more like a confession. A timetable." He tapped the manila envelope. "And this just arrived by special courier an hour ago. The authentication from my contacts at the Ministry of Culture in Rome. The analysis of the equipment in Carlo's cellar."

My breath caught. "And?"

He shrugged, a hard smile flickering across his lips. "It's exactly what we thought, but now it's official. The press, the labels, the inks, it's a professional-grade forgery operation, specifically for counterfeiting rare wine labels. They even identified a partial serial number on one of the presses that matches equipment reported stolen from a defunct print shop in Naples two years ago." He held up the envelope as if it were a shield. "This isn't just our theory anymore, Bianca. This is evidence. Hard, bureaucratic, Roman evidence. And now, combined with Maria's note..." He let the sentence hang, the implication clear.

He held up the envelope, and in that moment, surrounded by proof and shared purpose, the space between us vanished. He was no longer just my ally, he was the only person in the world who understood the weight of this, the danger and the hope. My hand found his, our fingers lacing together, the contact a silent vow.

The two pieces of paper, one cheap and terrified, the other official and damning, changed everything. Or so we hoped. The vague uneasiness of the evening solidified into a clear, urgent path. We were no longer just two meddlers with a suspicion.

"Marco can't dismiss this," I said, feeling a surge of defiant energy. "He can't tell us it's speculation or that we're in over our heads. Not with this."

"No, he can't," Enzo agreed, his voice firm with a new resolve. All hesitation, all patience, was gone, burned away by the raw fear on Maria's page and the facts in the envelope. "That's it. No more waiting. No more debating procedure." He carefully slipped Maria's note back into my hand. "We go to Marco. First thing in the morning. We show him all of it. The timeline, the motive, the official proof, and the plea from a witness inside Carlo's own house. We still have enough time to put a stop to this."

The performance was over. The waiting was done. Standing there in the dark alley, the decision felt less like a choice and more like an inevitable conclusion, the only path forward that Maria's courage and a bureaucrat in Rome had handed to us. We would go to Marco equals bearing undeniable proofs. The cozy comfort of my gelateria felt a world away, but for the first time since Claudio Vespucci collapsed there, I felt we were finally stepping out of the shadows and onto solid ground.

Chapter 15

Weight of Proof

Morning brought no peace, only a brittle, sleepless clarity. I opened Dolce Vita as usual, turned the key, drew up the blinds, polished the marble counter until the surface gleamed. My hands moved with the ghost of habit, but my mind was trapped in the opulent nightmare of the trattoria.

The black dress, a shield I'd worn with such determination, now hung in my closet feeling like a costume from a play that had taken a dangerous turn. Every time a customer walked in, I turned on a smile, pulled coffee, counted change, all the while watching the clock. Each minute was an eternity. Behind the chatter about weather and tourists, the whispers were still there: poison, scandal, shame. And through it all, one memory pressed hardest: Maria's trembling hand dropping the folded slip at dinner, as though passing me her own heartbeat.

Finally, at half-past nine, I could stop this pretense. I flipped the sign to 'Closed,' the slip of paper in my pocket feeling like it was burning a hole through the fabric. Enzo was already waiting outside the museum, his jacket slung over one arm, the stiff manila envelope containing Rome's verdict held securely under the other. His expression was set, the lines around his eyes deeper than usual. He looked like a man who had also spent the night staring at the ceiling, plotting moves on a chessboard that was tilting beneath us.

"We show him everything we have, whether he likes it or not," he said, his voice low and final. It was not a suggestion, but a battle plan.

Together, we walked to the station. The late morning in Cala d'Oro was filled with familiar, comforting sounds: the screeching of gulls wheeling over the harbor, a fisherman loudly grumbling about the day's poor catch, the rhythmic bang of shutters being flung open to welcome the day. Though ordinary, these noises now resonated with a strange, sharp urgency. Each sound felt like a tick of a clock counting down to nightfall.

We found Marco in his cramped, dimly lit office, the walls seeming to close in around the chaos of papers and reports scattered across his desk. His sleeves were rolled up to his elbows, and his tie hung loosely around his neck, as if he had already been wrestling with the demands of his day and already lost. The lines on his face and the weary look in his eyes told the story of a man burdened by too many responsibilities and too little sleep.

He looked up as our shadows fell across his doorway, and his expression, already strained, tightened with immediate irritation. "You again," he stated, the words a flat exhalation of annoyance. He made no move to welcome us, his body language a clear barrier. After a long, deliberate pause, he let out a sharp, dismissive sigh. "Bah. Fine. Make it quick." He gestured impatiently for us to enter the cluttered space, his voice heavy with a fatigue that seemed amplified by our presence. He did not offer us a seat.

Enzo didn't wait for permission. He stepped forward and laid the evidence on Marco's desk in three deliberate, damning movements. First, the photos from the trattoria cellar, the presses and molds captured vivid and illicit under the camera's flash. Then, he placed the stamped and signed response from the Ministry of Culture in Rome, the official letterhead a stark contrast to the messy desk. Finally, my hand trembling only slightly, I laid down Maria's folded note, its edge still faintly marked with kitchen oil, a tiny, human stain on the bureaucratic tableau.

Marco's eyes moved methodically from one page to the next, his expression neutral, betraying neither surprise nor interest. He picked up the stamped document, glanced at the seal, and set it down without comment. He gave the photos a cursory glance before his gaze settled on the handwritten note, which he read once, then again, his lips pressed in a thin line.

He finally leaned back, his chair emitting a soft groan. He steepled his fingers, his gaze settling not on the persons before him, but on the middle distance, as if weighing the evidence against a vast internal ledger.

"I see," he said, his tone not harsh, but weary and deeply unimpressed. "So, this is what we have."

He gestured toward the documents. "Photographs that show...objects in a location. They tell a story, but it's one that could be read a dozen different ways." His finger then tapped the official letter. "A stamp from a ministry. It lends an air of authority, I'll grant you that. But in my experience, a stamp confirms that a fee was paid or a form was filed, not that a truth was uncovered."

Finally, he picked up the handwritten note, holding it by the corner as if it were slightly distasteful. "And this. A statement from an eyewitness. A nervous one, by your own admission." He set it down carefully. "Her account is...emotionally compelling. But it's the account of someone who was frightened. Fear has a way of reshaping what the eyes actually see."

He let out a long, slow breath, a man burdened by the follies of others. "Look. I understand why you brought this to me. It paints a picture. But it's a picture painted on a shaky canvas. There's no chain of custody for these items, no secondary verification, no credible witness without a vested interest."

He met our eyes, his gaze firm but not cruel. "As I told you earlier, as it stands, this isn't proof. What you assembled is still just a collection of suspicions. To act on this alone would be...well, it would be unprofessional the least."

He paused, letting the finality of those words settle. Yet, his posture remained, suggesting his dismissal was not the end of the conversation, but a challenge to it. As I saw it, he had stated his position. The ball was now in our court to convince him why he should lower his professional standards and engage with what he clearly saw as flimsy evidence.

A hot spike of anger pierced through my anxiety. "They're not nothing," my voice cutting sharper than I intended. "They're date. Location. Ettore threatened me because Carlo is moving them *tonight*. At Lazzaro. And Maria, his own niece, risked everything to give us this." I leaned forward, palms flat on the edge of his desk, the memory of Carlo's veiled threats and Maria's terror lending a new, urgent heat to my words. "And that 'junk' is what Benedetti wants cleared out by morning. He will cover his tracks before the sun comes up. You told us to bring you facts. Here they are."

Enzo's voice continued, steady and purposeful, a rock against the tide of Marco's skepticism. "Marco, *you* wanted facts beyond mere gossip. This is your chance. These are facts, however your 'procedure' sees them. If you wait, Carlo will be gone and the evidence with him. Move tonight, and you'll catch him red-handed with the crates and decide for yourself. This is no longer just a theory in our heads. It is an actionable tip with a deadline."

Marco sighed, a long, weary exhalation. He pressed his thumbs against his eyes, as if grinding away a headache born of our persistence. When he lowered his hands, he looked older than any of us, his ambition exhausted by the grinding apathy of small-town policing. When he spoke, it was with the voice of a parent forced to indulge a child's elaborate fantasy, resigned to the inevitable disappointment. "Alright." The word was a concession, heavy with reluctance. "Two officers. Not a squad. The harbor patrol boat, if I can borrow it without raising alarms. We keep it quiet. If this is nothing, I take the heat. If it's real, the report stays clean — no mention of you.

You understand? You stay out of it from this moment on."

Relief washed through me, sudden and electric, so potent it made my knees feel weak. Enzo's nod was barely perceptible, but in the context of his stoic reserve, it might as well have been a shouted victory cry.

But as we walked out of the oppressive office and into the sharp, bright sunlight of the *piazza*, the relief quickly turned bitter. The sun felt too harsh, the air too thin. I found myself shaking, a fine tremor that had nothing to do with the fresh mid-morning air. Doubt came back, pressing at the back of my throat. Would Marco truly follow through? Or would today's promises, like so much else in this town, vanish into the same stack of neglected files that littered his desk, victims of convenience and fear?

We split ways at the fountain, agreeing to meet after dark, a plan that now felt terrifyingly fragile. I walked back to the gelateria alone, the carefree sounds of the town now feeling like a mockery. We had handed Marco everything, and he had agreed to act. So why did it feel like we had just jumped from the frying pan and were now waiting to see if the fire below was real or just another illusion?

***

I spent the afternoon in a daze, half-working the gelateria, but barely processing the customers. Every time the bell above the door jingled, I expected someone to step in and declare everything exposed. Instead, the day unfolded with cruel normalcy: children pressed tacky coins to the glass, tourists posed for photos, and Lucia, knowing nothing for her own safety, regaled me with some story about her nephew's wedding. I nodded, smiled, and measured out scoops by rote, every sense tuned to the ticking of the clock behind the register.

When closing time came, I couldn't remember a single flavor I'd served. My mind was already at Punta Seca, running through the plan, picturing Maria's face when she learned what we'd done.

Our meeting point was a sturdy walk, secluded by a ring of limestone and accessible only by a narrow footpath choked with wild rosemary and gorse. I arrived early, the sound of the sea flattening all other noise. From the bluff I could see the outline of the boathouse, its roof patched with corrugated tin, and beyond it, the black shimmer of the water. I noticed the harbor patrol boat was in place already, quiet, its running lights off, a shadow among shadows, for now silent and dark, the outline barely visible.

Marco's men moved into position: one hidden in brush along the land path, another stationed by the wild olive grove bend. The three of us, Marco, Enzo, and I, crouched on the bluff above the boathouse, the structure hunched at the tide's edge, roof sloping toward the sea. The air was heavy with tar and seaweed. Time dragged, the waves whispering in and out, until each creak of wood inside the boathouse made gave me a jolt.

Just after midnight, movement broke the stillness. Ettore emerged first, limping but steady, hauling one end of a heavy crate. On the opposite corner, a younger man, hunched, unfamiliar, his features obscured by shadow, dug his feet into the shingle, both men grunting from the weight. They guided the crate down a path worn by years of salt and foot traffic, then carefully dropped it, the impact echoing up the limestone bluff to where we waited, bodies tensed and faces drawn sharp in the May night chill.

Moonlight caught the stenciling: LZ-47.

Within five minutes, Ettore and his accomplice reemerged hauling another — LZ-48. This time, the younger man's resolve wavered and the box slipped, landing hard and splitting the edge.

Straw and sawdust erupted from the split wood, dancing in the night air as something caught the moonlight, unmistakable glint of metal plates within. We saw a flash of blue against the white glimmer of moon, some official insignia or stamp, maybe, or else a scrap of cloth tangled in the packing. Hard to say at this distance, but the intent was obvious: these were not artifacts bound for restoration or display, but the very implements of the forgery itself I had seen in Benedetti's trattoria cellar.

We heard suddenly Carlo, ever the taskmaster, barking instructions sounding like curses to both of them in a low, guttural dialect even Marco struggled to interpret. The younger man, hands shaking badly, kept darting glances over his shoulder as if looking for someone to help him.

The moment stretched until time itself seemed to liquefy. "Valli, with me," Marco whispered, already moving toward the quay, signaling the officers hidden below. The plan was simple, effective, and silent until it could be silent no longer.

From opposite ends of the cove, shadows materialized, officers moving with grim efficiency, boots muffled by sand and moss. At the same moment, oars from the patrol boat churned the water into a brief froth, propelling the black hull up against the rocks to block any escape by sea. Ettore caught the movement first; his head snapped up, eyes wild in the lantern light. The knife appeared as if conjured from his sleeve, the blade a pale crescent against the dark.

"Drop it!" Marco bellowed, gun raised.

Ettore roared, swinging his knife in a wild arc that sent the nearest officer stumbling back. The shadows from the floodlights jittered across the rocks, stretching his figure into something monstrous. For a brief instant, it seemed more like an eerie presence than a battle, with his fury so intense that it seemed to slice through the very fabric of the night.

I scrambled down the bluff, gravel biting into my palms. My breath hitched as Ettore snarled, his blade flashing toward the younger officer. The crates rattled as he stumbled back, and for a heartbeat I thought Ettore might break through. Marco's pistol cracked skyward, the sound tearing the night apart. Gulls screamed, the cove alive with wings and panic. Ettore froze, then howled as Marco slammed him into the stones, his arm twisted until the knife fell.

Carlo wasn't running.

With a snarl, he wrenched a fuel canister from the prepared skiff's motor mount, the metal clanging as he dragged it across the stones. He yanked the cap loose and upended it in one swift motion, sending a reeking tide of gasoline sloshing over the stacked crates. The sharp stench clawed my throat, and I saw the sheen spreading fast across the boards of the boathouse floor.

"Back!" Carlo roared, his voice ragged but triumphant. "One spark, and it all goes — the crates, the proof, this whole damn shack."

He snapped a lighter to life, the small flame licking at the dark. The sight of it against the timber made my stomach clench.

"Carlo!" Marco shouted, his voice cutting hard across the cove. "Drop it. Don't do this. The cannery burned because of you once, you think the town will forget if you try again?"

Carlo's smile was thin and savage, his teeth catching the light. "Rumors! Nobody can prove anything and...and they forgot once before anyway. They'll forget again. Ash doesn't talk."

He angled the lighter toward the nearest crate, the fire dancing hungrily. The flame winked in his hand, and for a split second I saw Ettore's knife glinting in the alley, Maria's hand shaking as she passed the note to me. Warnings had been building toward this moment, each one daring me to look away. Stones slid under my boots as I lunged forward — a move that shocked Marco, Enzo *and* Carlo, and even me. My shoulder connected with his arm, and under the sudden pressure the canister and the lighter flew from his grip. The canister bounced across the rocks with a hollow clatter before coming to rest at the water's edge, where waves lapped at the last of its spilling contents, while the lighter spun from his fingers, skittering into the tide. My shoulder hit the ground, the impact rattling my breath from my chest.

Two officers lunged, dragging him down, snapping iron on his wrists as he thrashed and spat.

The cove fell still, save for the stink of fuel and the slap of waves. Ettore writhed, cursing under the weight of another officer. The crates loomed slick with gasoline, silent and waiting, the floodlight glaring over them like a verdict.

Carlo lifted his head, his hair sticking to his face, and his burning eyes fixed on me. "Do you really think it ends here?" His voice grated like a blade against stone. "You haven't stopped anything. Just wait." A sudden chill ran through me that had nothing to do with the night air, though I told myself it was only the chill of the sea breeze against my sticky skin.

On the stones, Marco worked with meticulous calm, his every movement a counterpoint to the chaos that had just ripped through the cove. He photographed each crate, recorded the numbers, and had the officers seal them with the precision of ritual. The open one lay exposed under the floodlight, counterfeit plates packed in straw, their faintly crooked serial marks a perfect match as confirmed by the Rome specialists.

Enzo crouched beside it, sleeves rolled, lamplight catching on the first silver at his temples. His eyes narrowed as he examined the metal plates, speaking with quiet intensity. "These forgery tools — such precision, such artistry. The hands that made these could have created masterpieces instead of criminal instruments." He exhaled slowly, a sound weighted with genuine regret and disappointment only a historian could feel at a moment like this.

I stood a little apart, still heaving a little, my hands still trembling as the salt air rasped in my lungs. The stench of spilled fuel still clung to the night. My shoulder throbbed from where I'd hit the ground, but what lingered most was Carlo's gaze. He sat cuffed and sweating, his shirt plastered to him, his eyes locked on me with something between fury and a dark promise.

Ettore was silent now, pinned and sullen, the fight drained from him. "He hasn't been family to me in years," Marco stated flatly, his eyes on the cuffed man seething quietly in the dirt. "Not since my father threw him out of the house for stealing from his own brother."

For some time I'd half-believed the badge on Marco's uniform was only another mask. But when I heard him, when he spat Ettore's name like that, I felt the knot I'd been carrying finally uncoil. He wasn't covering. He was fighting. And for the first time, I trusted him without reservation.

The sea breathed on, steady and indifferent, as if mocking the human noise.

A shadow fell across me, warm where the floodlight was cold. Enzo. He didn't speak right away. His hand hovered as if to reach for mine, then he settled instead on brushing damp hair from my face, his touch gentle, almost reverent.

"You could have been burned alive," he murmured, his voice tight but low enough for only me. "Bianca...what you did—" He broke off, searching my eyes, not for answers but for reassurance that I was still standing in front of him.

I tried to laugh, but it came out cracked. "You sound like *Zia* Lucia!"

"Ah! Lucia would scold. I..." He exhaled, the fight gone from his shoulders. "I don't know what I'd do if you hadn't pushed that can away. And the lighter..."

The words caught me off guard, loosening something in my chest that the fear had locked tight. For a moment, the scene around us, the officers, the crates, Marco's orders, faded, and there was only his hand still at my temple, his eyes dark and unguarded.

"You don't have to worry," I replied gently, though my voice shook. "I'm still here."

He gave a short, rueful laugh, as if I had missed the point. “That’s exactly why I’ll worry.”

The tide slapped against the stones, indifferent, eternal. But when Enzo’s thumb lingered at my cheek, rough with the faint scrape of callus and ink, I felt a steadiness returning, as though the ground itself had decided not to give way under me.

And even as Carlo was dragged past us, his voice was a low stream of venom, Enzo shifted slightly closer. His shoulder brushed mine, a silent anchor, making the night survivable. As Marco’s men hauled him toward the waiting car, Carlo suddenly went still. He turned his head, and his eyes, piercing and flat, found me in the gloom. All the bluster was gone, replaced by a terrifying calm.

“A word of advice from a businessman to a Milanese girl,” his voice so smooth it was more threatening than any shout. “You may believe you’ve won a battle tonight, but you’ve stepped into a war far *far* beyond this little seaside town. The people I work with operate on a scale you can’t imagine! And I can promise you this — they never forget a face...”

He let the words hang, a promise etched in ice. Then he was shoved into the car. The door slammed shut, sealing the threat inside. A chill passed through me, and this time I could not lie to myself. This cold had nothing to do with the sea. The night suddenly felt quieter, the victory smaller. His words painted a picture of a network that stretched far beyond this cove, and I had just put myself right in the middle of it.

Chapter 16

When Morning Broke

By dawn, Cala d'Oro stirred to life in the way only a fishing town could: shutters banging open, gulls shrieking for scraps, the smell of brine sharper than coffee. But this morning felt heavier. Patrol cars idled along the quay, their lights dim but their presence undeniable. Gossip that usually took half a day to ripple through the *piazza* had already spread before the sun cleared the rooftops.

Word had gone out last night, and by dawn every soul in town felt it like a grit between the teeth: Carlo Benedetti had been taken in, and the police were searching his family's trattoria for evidence.

Marco looked worn out, shirt creased, jaw rough with stubble, eyes shadowed from the long night at the boathouse. Yet his stride was steady as he led his officers into the Benedetti trattoria.

The front door was already unlocked, Maria Benedetti having surrendered the keys with the flat, resigned dignity of someone who was doing a difficult, but the right thing. Marco gave her a nod, polite, but not warm, and gestured for a colleague to take her statement. Maria hesitated, then turned away, her footsteps heavy on the stairs.

Marco had made it clear already before dawn: Enzo and I weren't there as spectators. We were part of the main thread that had unraveled Carlo's scheme. Enzo's archival work had given the coded lists their meaning, and my photos and the date from Maria'a note had drawn the line straight to the trattoria. "You've both earned your place in this case," Marco had said gruffly, ignoring the skeptical looks from his officers. "Stay back when I say so, but I want the truth to come out clean — and fast."

That was why, when the cellar doors groaned open and the thick air wrapped around us, he didn't wave us off. He needed more than evidence, he also needed Maria to talk. And Marco also sensed, perhaps better than anyone, that she would only unburden herself if she saw a trusted face.

As the cellar opened, the air inside was musty, sour with cork dust and mildew. The walls were stacked high with bottles, more than any family could drink in a lifetime. Most were local labels, the sort you could buy in bulk at the open market, but there were also pricey French imports and Italian reserves, the kind tourists posed with for pictures. The light showed long shelves, displaying a pattern of dust and the subtle rearrangements, scuffed patches where bottles had been shifted, new cardboard shims wedged between old wood. He knew how to read a cellar. This was not just storage, it was staging. The stack of crates in the corner drew Marco's eye.

He pulled one open. Instead of wine, the straw concealed a neat array of tools: a handheld corking device, a cutter for foil caps, solvent bottles with their chemical smell sharp enough to sting. Empty glass bottles — expensive Burgundy shapes, imported Bordeaux — gleamed faintly in the gloom, waiting to be dressed as something they were not.

Marco rifled through a small wooden chest beside the stack and drew out a battered notebook, its pages filled with Carlo's cramped hand. Unlike the museum ledger, this was no relic, it was current, weeks and months laid out in columns. Each entry matched a date and a code to a quantity of bottles moved, always in lots of twelve or twenty-four, never less. Some entries were circled, others crossed out in red. He recognized a few names, including the mayor's own cousin and a well-known hotelier, both listed as "delivery." In the margins, code words for cash drops and payment schedules. At a glance it matched the note Ettore had carried, and the movements Maria would later describe in the note she passed to me.

The snap of the notebook closing echoed off the cellar walls. “Enough to show intent,” Marco said flatly. “And to prove this cellar wasn’t just an ordinary trattoria storage.”

At first, Maria shrank into the shadows as the officers shifted crates and logged finds. Her arms wrapped around herself, her jaw clenched tight. I caught her eye, but she looked away quickly, as if the weight of it would crush her if she met my gaze.

Then Enzo stepped closer, not looming, but folding himself gently into her line of sight with the same calm he used on nervous donors at the museum.

“Maria,” he said, his voice warm, steady. “We’re here because we know what you risked, writing that note. You can trust us with the rest.”

She looked at him, then at me. For a long moment she said nothing, her lips pressed tight, until at last her gaze softened. “I didn’t know who else to turn to,” she whispered. “Uncle has everyone here under his thumb. If I had gone to the police, he would have heard before I finished the sentence. But you —” she faltered, then swallowed hard. “That day at the trattoria, I saw you come up from the cellar. The look on your face...you knew. You had seen something. And I thought, you were the only one who wasn't part of his world, the only one who might understand what was happening.” A flicker of something like hope crossed her face. "And I heard what you did in Milan, how you stood up in court. You weren't afraid. That's why I slipped you the note. And *Zia* Lucia...she always said your grandmother could be trusted. So I thought maybe you could be too."

Her lips parted as though something dammed inside her finally cracked. A shudder ran through her, and she sank onto a crate as if her legs had simply given up.

"I was always helping move these," she whispered. "Uncle said it was just wine. That the press was for display. But after Vespucci..."

Marco crouched to meet her eyes, his voice softer now. "You did the right thing, *ragazza,* you were very brave. Tell us everything."

And she did. Her voice trembled at first, then steadied as confession brought relief. She spoke of Carlo's herb collection in the cellar — the bitter roots, the fennel, the wormwood he used in his recipes. Then her eyes darkened. "Few days before Vespucci came for lunch, I watched my uncle bring in oleander branches, flowers, leaves and all. Pink flowers, so pretty. He boiled them and put the liquid in a jar with the rest." Maria's fingers knotted in her apron. "And then, when...when Vespucci ordered our seafood stew special, I saw him adding something from this jar. 'For color,' he told me then with a wink when he noticed I was watching him." She looked up, her face hollow with guilt. "I knew better, but I stayed silent. I should have —," tears started rolling down her face.

Marco said nothing, he just looked up from his notes with a thoughtful look on his face. "Anything else you remember, warnings, names, something someone said."

Maria wiped her eyes, her brow furrowing in concentration. "There was...an argument. In the kitchen, about a week before it happened. Vespucci was there, his voice low and angry. I only caught a piece of it as I passed by the door. He said to my uncle, '...buried at Lazzaro. You think I won't dig it up? I'll ruin you.' I didn't understand it then. I thought it was just another business quarrel. But now..." Her voice trailed off, the new horror dawning on her.

She twisted the corner of her handkerchief. "Uncle likes to turn stories into warnings," she said. "I once heard him telling Ettore not to make Matteo's mistake. He never said straight what that mistake was, only that Matteo paid for it with his life in the cannery fire. He repeats it often, like a lesson."

"Why tell Ettore that?" Marco asked.

"Because Ettore was pushing too far, I think," she said carefully. "I don't know the details, only that Uncle was shouting. A crate had been left in the wrong alley, someone had seen it, and Uncle was furious.

He told Ettore that Matteo's mistake was carelessness too, and he wouldn't tolerate another."

Her fingers knotted the handkerchief tighter. "That was when I realized...if he could use death of Ettore's brother as a warning, then no one was safe, not even me. I'd seen and heard too much. So I wrote the note and passed it to *Signora* Bianca. Just in case...before it was too late, in case something happened to me too." Her eyes flickered, haunted.

Marco snapped his notebook shut, his jaw taut. "Show me the jar," he said gently, but firmly.

Maria rose on unsteady legs and led us deeper into the cellar, past the crates and empty bottles, to a low shelf at the back. There, half hidden behind jars of dried citrus peel and star anise, stood a glass bottle filled with a dark amber liquid. The glass was smudged with fingerprints, the cork stained. Even from a step away, the bitter, medicinal odor made my stomach lurch.

"That one," Maria whispered, backing away. "That's the one."

Marco lifted it carefully with a gloved hand, holding it up to the light. "You're sure?"

She nodded, arms wrapped tight around herself.

Marco's eyes met mine, the implication hanging in the air between us. "I don't think this was ever meant for a kitchen," he stated, his voice flat and professional. He labeled the jar himself, marking it for urgent transport to Ancona.

The confirmation came via a stark email hours later: positive for cardiac glycosides. A perfect match for the oleander traces in Vespucci's system.

"The timeline fits," Marco explained when he stopped by, the facts clicking into place like tumblers in a lock. "The poison was administered at lunch, it just took its time. His collapse in your shop later afternoon was a terrible coincidence."

The chain was complete. It was Carlo's "seafood special", that Vespucci had eaten few hours before his collapse in my gelateria, not my gelato.

The gelato, retested twice, was clean.

"I went back through the cannery fire file," Marco finally added. "The investigators noted a strong solvent odor near the loading bay, but without a suspect they left the cause undetermined. They logged Matteo Rossi among the dead and closed it as an accident." He set the notebook flat on the table. "Now, with the payroll anomalies and log inconsistencies decoded, those old notes read differently. It looks less like bad luck, more like deliberate fire-setting, seems arson was the probable cause."

By afternoon the trattoria was sealed, evidence logged, Maria as a crucial witness under quiet protection. I returned to Dolce Vita as though stepping back into a forgotten life.

At dusk, when the *piazza* glowed gold and the sea began its slow darkening. I stood at the polished counter, slicing blood oranges with methodical precision. I felt the muscles in my arms relax for the first time in weeks, the skin beneath my apron no longer prickling with the dread of being watched, judged, suspected. With every clean cut, I found myself reclaiming the small, ordinary joys I'd lost to the investigation — the citrus mist on my fingers, the subtle pleasure of a well-packed cone, the simple act of serving another without having any second thoughts. Maybe tomorrow I will try folding basil into apricot puree, or slip saffron into citrus. Nonna never stuck to vanilla I mused, and I liked to think I was only keeping her curiosity alive.

I heard his footsteps before I saw him. Slow, steady, unhurried, they threaded through the hum of voices and the clink of glasses until he reached the counter. The golden evening light caught his face in warm tones, softening the sharpness of the day.

He leaned lightly on the wood, close enough that I could catch the faint trace of salt and paper clinging to him. His smile was different this time, unguarded, free of the shadows it had carried for weeks.

"It's good to see you smiling again," he said quietly. "It's over now, Bianca. You can breathe."

I tried to answer with a joke, something flippant to keep the exchange light, but as I opened my mouth, the words tangled with something raw. All at once I felt my eyes sting, my throat tighten. The world hadn't shifted, not really, but for the first time in a long time I let go. I pressed both palms to the counter, grounding myself in the hard marble, and let myself feel the full, dizzy relief.

"Only because you were here."

For a moment we simply looked at each other. Around us the square carried on children shouting, waiters balancing trays, music spilling from the cafés, but it felt distant, blurred at the edges.

I watched him as he watched me, we both aware of the strange gravity that had formed between us since it all began. I thought of the hours I'd spent hunched over ledgers, tracing the looping threads, each time I was frightened and ready to give up and how it was Enzo, not just my own stubbornness, that had pulled me back each time.

What was near, what was steady, was him.

I drew a breath, let it out slowly. "You weren't just standing beside me, Enzo. You helped me put the pieces together when everything felt impossible. You kept me from losing myself in it."

His eyes held mine, unflinching. “With you,” he said softly, “I never doubted we’d reach the truth.”

I felt my pulse leap, and for the first time in years I didn’t try to silence it. I let the words rise, even as my cheeks flared with color, expressing emotions never my strong side. “You matter more than I ever expected.”

His expression gentled, the guarded tension I had grown used to was gone. “And you matter more to me than you realize,” he said, quiet but certain.

We stood like that for a while, the world spinning gently around us, neither willing to break the spell. Then he reached across the marble counter, his fingers finding mine among the scattered orange peels. Then he lifted my hand, his touch was gentle, as if I were something precious he’d searched for his whole life. His lips brushed my skin, warm, certain. The touch was fleeting, the gesture was simple, yet it carried the weight of everything unspoken between us.

Outside, Cala d’Oro carried on, laughter, music, the sea whispering against the stones, but as the sky reflected the sparkling day, I felt as though the whole town exhaled with me.

Epilogue

"Two scoops of pistachio, please. Nonna says it's good for the soul."

The boy couldn't have been older than seven, his elbows barely clearing the counter. He pushed a sticky coin across the glass with the solemnity of a bank transfer, eyes wide with urgency.

I smiled as I handed him the cone. "Your Nonna's a very wise woman."

He grinned, snatched the ice cream, and ran off, legs flying. At the fountain, his grandmother sat with her cane hooked on the edge of the stone. She steadied him with one hand and caught my eye, giving a nod that was not just polite but grateful. For the first time in weeks, I didn't see suspicion in someone's gaze — only thanks.

The day moved forward on that note. Cones passed across the counter, laughter floated in through the open door, and Lucia kept her post at the entrance, half gossiping with customers, half watching over me with the vigilance of a hawk disguised as a silver-haired matriarch. The rhythm of ordinary life was back, fragile but real.

Marco stopped by that afternoon. He ordered *stracciatella*, as he had a hundred times before, but this time he paid with exact change, deliberately dropping the coins into the tip jar. A small gesture, but pointed. He lingered longer than usual, his eyes following the steady line of customers stretching toward the square.

"They'll stay put for now," he said quietly, as if finishing a conversation we had started some time before. "Carlo's been transferred to Genoa. The homicide charge is the priority, the prosecutor is building the case now. Once the toxicology report is officially finalized, it's a done deal. They'll add the fraud charges to show motive and pattern — it's what will ensure he never sees the outside of a prison again. Ettore...well, he broke quickly and talked," he said. "He confirmed the workshop was in the cannery loft years ago. The fire wasn't an accident, Matteo Rossi torched it after a quarrel, and most of the operation went with the rafters. Carlo rebuilt later, somewhere else. We're still piecing together where, but the local cache in the Benedetti's cellar you uncovered, proves the trade never stopped."

A sudden melancholy sharpened Marco's features, his jaw working in silence.

"Ettore is my uncle, the family's black sheep. Blood or not, he signed his statement. He was sentenced to multiple years for assault and for his role in a counterfeiting scheme. He also gave up the 'Ravenna contact' — the 'C.' in the ledger. Turns out it was a middleman for auction houses in Milan, but that's a separate investigation now, led by a different unit. The court will take its time, but neither of them will be walking Cala d'Oro's streets again anytime soon. That much I can promise you."

By nightfall the cannery fire would stop being a rumor and become a line in a report, signed and filed. Marco didn't look pleased, he shook his head in a gesture of resignation rather than victory. "It's done," he said. "Finally."

Relief loosened something I hadn't realized I was still holding tight. Marco — the boy who'd once raced me down these same streets, who'd grown up to wear a uniform I wasn't sure I could trust — was exactly what I'd hoped. Honest. Steady. What a policeman should be. I hadn't misjudged him.

As if to soften the weight of his words, Marco tapped the counter with his knuckles. "Best gelato in town. Don't let anyone tell you otherwise." Then he turned, his uniform catching the last of the *piazza's* light as he stepped outside. A little girl darted in past him, coins clutched in her fist, eager for her turn at the counter.

For a moment, it felt ordinary again. Blessedly ordinary. This was what I had wanted all along: quiet days, the comfort of routine, a chance to breathe.

I closed the gelateria that night, the motions a well-practiced ritual. Lucia was waiting outside, as if she had known the precise moment the last customer would leave. She slipped her arm through mine without asking, steering me toward the square.

"You held up well, *ragazza*," she said, brisk as always, but with warmth in her eyes. "Better than most would have. Your Nonna would be proud."

That caught me off guard, tightening my throat. I squeezed her arm in thanks, not trusting myself to speak.

We passed the fountain where workers balanced on ladders, stringing lanterns across balconies. Bright red, gold, green and pale blue shells bobbed gently overhead, waiting for their night to shine. Children chasing beneath them, laughing as they tried to swat the dangling cords.

Lucia slowed. "They've started early this year," she murmured. "When the festival comes, nothing in this town stays quiet for long."

She didn't explain, and I didn't ask. Her arm stayed linked with mine, steady as ever, while the lanterns swayed above us, bright against the darkening sky. I told myself she meant the noise and the music, the clamor of celebration. But part of me wasn't so sure.

The lanterns rippled in the breeze, lovely and fragile, promising joy, and yet I couldn't shake the thought that they looked just as much like omens. Shadows dressed in light, waiting for their moment.

Italian Glossary

For the curious, a short glossary of the Italian terms used in this book below, just as you might hear them spoken in the *piazza* or at a gelateria counter in Cala d'Oro. While these words and phrases are not essential to follow the story, they have been included to add a touch of local color to evoke as much as possible the authentic atmosphere and the feeling of being in Cala d'Oro.

Amarena: sour cherry, classic gelato flavor made with sour cherries

Aperto / Chiuso: open / closed, common signs seen on shop doors

Bagno: bathroom (restroom)

Bene: literally "good," used to affirm or agree, similar to saying "all right" or "OK"

Biscotti: literally "twice-baked," traditional Italian almond cookies, crisp and oblong, often dunked in coffee or sweet wine

Bombolone / bomboloni: Italian doughnut(s), round, sugar-dusted pastries, usually filled with cream, custard, or jam, often enjoyed with morning coffee

Branzino: sea bass

Brava: literally "good" or "well done" (feminine form), used to praise or encourage someone

Buongiorno: good morning

Cala d'Oro: "Golden Cove," name of the town, literally "cove of gold"

Cannolo / cannoli: Sicilian pastry consisting of a fried tube of dough filled with sweetened ricotta cream

Cantuccio / cantucci: crunchy almond biscuit(s) from Tuscany, often dipped in dessert wine, or these days also coffee

Cara: literally "dear," affectionate term used to address a woman

Carabiniere / carabinieri: member(s) of Italy's national gendarmerie, a branch of the armed forces with civilian police duties. Often distinguished from the *polizia* by their uniforms and military structure

Chianti: famous Tuscan red wine

Cornetto / Cornetti: croissant-style pastry, typical Italian breakfast pastry in the shop

Culatello: prized cured meat from Parma, made from the hind leg of the pig, similar to prosciutto but aged and considered more delicate

Dio mio: literally "my God," an exclamation of surprise, frustration, or disbelief

Dolce Vita: "sweet life", but also a cultural phrase

Espresso: strong coffee shot, sipped typically after lunch

Faccia della terra: "face of the earth", idiom: fall off the face of the earth

Fiore di latte: literally "flower of milk," classic gelato made with milk, sugar, and cream, with a delicate dairy taste.

Gelataia: feminine form of gelato maker

Gelato: Italian-style ice cream, characterized by a denser texture and less fat than traditional ice cream

Gelateria: gelato shop, selling Italian-style ice cream, granitas, pastries and coffee

Granita: Sicilian-style shaved ice served with a sweet syrup dessert

La ragazza con lo sguardo affilato: the girl with the sharp gaze

La Repubblica: one of Italy's major daily newspapers, known for its national coverage and investigative reporting

Lazzaro del Mare: "Lazarus of the Sea"

Linguine: type of long flat pasta, served often with clams

Maraffa: traditional Italian card game, especially popular in Emilia-Romagna, fast-paced trick-taking game, often played with lively banter and small wagers, and is a common sight in village cafés and piazzas

Museo del Mare: Museum of the Sea, the maritime museum in town

Nocciola: hazelnut, a classic gelato flavor

Nero d'Avola: famous Sicilian red wine

Nonna: grandmother

Occupato!: occupied!

Pasta e fagioli: traditional Italian soup made with pasta and beans, usually in a tomato-based broth, considered rustic comfort food

Pasticceria: pastry shop or bakery specializing in sweets, cakes, and pastries

Pistacchio: pistachio, popular gelato flavor, spelled the Italian way here

Piazza: town square, central social space of the village

Primo: literally "first," in Italian dining, it refers to the **first course**, usually pasta, risotto, or soup

Procura: short for *Procura della Repubblica*, the public prosecutor's office in Italy, responsible for directing investigations and bringing criminal cases to court

Ragazza: girl, young woman

Sfogliatella: layered shell-shaped pastry from Naples, crisp outside with a ricotta-based filling

Signor: Mr., a formal address for a man

Signora: Mrs., a formal address for a woman

Signorina: Miss, a formal address for an unmarried woman

Sirocco: hot Sahara wind powerful enough to snap awnings

Stai attenta: be careful, watch yourself

Stracciatella: gelato flavour with small pieces of dark chocolate

Stronzo / stronzi: an insult, often translated as "fool", used in frustration or anger

Terrazzo: typical design of speckled stone flooring

Torta della nonna: grandmother's tart, custard tart with pine nuts served as dessert

Trattoria: Italian restaurant

Tutto: all, everything

Vicolo: narrow alley or side street, often found in historic Italian towns

Vongole: clams, as in linguine alle vongole dish

Zia: aunt, a respectful or affectionate form of address, used not only for family but also for older women in the community

Your Neighbours in Cala d'Oro

Bianca Moretti, once a high-flying forensic finance consultant in Milan, has returned to Cala d'Oro to take over her late Nonna's gelateria, Dolce Vita. She experiments with unusual flavors (some loved, some whispered about), walks the sea shore for shells, and tries to keep her life simple...until murder interrupts.

Lucia is known to all as *Zia* Lucia. From her kitchen window or over a jar of pickled vegetables, she dispenses gossip, advice, and sharp observations that travel faster than the church bells. If there's a secret in town, chances are she's heard it first.

Enzo Valli is a maritime historian with a fondness for tinkering on his old Alfa Romeo. He collects maps, writes in elegant calligraphy, and has the kind of sharp eye that can spot a forged signature, or a clue most would miss.

Inspector Marco Rossi is Cala d'Oro's police inspector, steady and stubborn, carrying both the authority of the badge and the shadows of his family past. His uneasy alliance with Bianca might just be something more.

Carlo Benedetti is the owner of a fancy trattoria just off the *piazza*, smooth on the surface, but with ties that go deeper into the town's history than he likes to admit.

Maria Benedetti is Carlo's niece, sharp-eyed and quick, often moving quietly in the background, but noticing far more than she lets on.

Ettore Rossi is Marco's uncle, limping through town with a reputation that keeps most neighbors at a careful distance.

Matteo Rossi was Marco's late uncle. His name is rarely spoken aloud, yet his shadow still lingers over Cala d'Oro.

And then there are the fishermen who mend their nets on the quay, the children pressing coins into Bianca's hand for gelato, and the tourists who think this town is nothing more than orange trees and sunlit *piazzas*.

You'll meet them all again soon, in new mysteries from Cala d'Oro, where the sea, the *piazza*, and even the gelato hold clues waiting to be uncovered.

Thanks for reading!

If you enjoyed this book, please leave a short review helping other readers find it.

The mystery in Cala d'Oro is never truly over...

The lanterns are rising, the piazza is glowing with festival cheer... but in ***Murder at the Lantern Festival***, Cala d'Oro's most beloved celebration hides a darker truth.

Bianca Moretti is caught in the middle, determined to uncover the truth.

Then comes ***Murder at the Palazzo***. When an American expat buys the town's crumbling palazzo, he stirs up secrets that were meant to stay buried.

Some walls hold more than history, and Bianca must face the shadows of Cala d'Oro's past before they claim another life.

For news, updates, and special treats from Cala d'Oro, such as *rosemary-pear* gelato recipe, visit:

www.victoriaamarin.com

Printed in Dunstable, United Kingdom

78729259R00129